Lost in Chance

Lost in Chance

Lize Jacobs

ISBN: 978-0-620-67791-2
Print Edition

Lize Jacobs Publishing
773, 31st Avenue
Villieria, 0186
South Africa

www.lizejacobs.com

Recently divorced teacher, Chrisna, is stuck in her small-town life in South Africa.

One day, she angrily tells her best friend that she would like to throw her wedding ring off the top of the Eiffel Tower. So her friend gifts her a five-day trip to Paris, for her thirtieth birthday, to do just that.

Unsure of whether she would actually be able to do it, she sets off, unprepared for the life-changing adventure, quirky new friend, and romance that await her, as she gets lost in chance.

For my dad.

Table of Contents

A heartfelt, gigantic, indescribable THANK YOU to:

My wonderful mom who supports my dreams
without question.

My talented brother, who challenges me and makes me
want to be better.

My best friend, Nadia, for being who you are.
Zedia Forever!

Sylvia and Trudie for your unwavering support.

Pieter, for the creative embryo that grew into this book.

Sue-Marie, for all your help, chica!

Beatrix, Mariane, and Liezl for always believing that I
could do this.

Mathilda, Willem, Elene, Christa and Christa.

Sumien and Melanie, my adopted sisters.

The best family in the world.

All my friends, who enrich my life daily. You know who
you are!

The spouses who put up with me.

My amazing publishing team; David, Lizette, Colette.

One

Was she falling, or was the ground pushing up to meet her?

She caught a glimpse of the Eiffel Tower disappearing behind the billowing clouds as her body twirled through the sky. A ray of light reflected off the gold band around her left ring finger, blinding her as she woke with a start.

Chrisna shuffled upright in the chair, and glanced around to see if anyone was looking at her, but no one was paying her any attention.

After buttoning the top button of her fitted gray sweater and straightening her black-rim glasses, she tried to tidy the long dark brown strands that had wiggled themselves out of her ponytail.

Pushing her index finger in underneath her glasses, she rubbed the sleep from her eyes and checked the time on her wristwatch, 2.15pm. She turned cold.

For a second, she sat frozen in her seat, and then she heard a female voice coming over the intercom system. "This is the final boarding call for passenger C. du Plessis, booked on flight 372BA to Paris. Please proceed to

Gate 10 immediately. I repeat. This is the final boarding call…"

Grabbing her bulky brown purse, which had served as a pillow, she unzipped the side pocket and pulled out her passport and boarding pass. She flung the strap over her shoulder and torpedoed down the corridor of Heathrow Terminal 5, toward Gate 10.

Frantic and out of breath, she handed the boarding gate attendant her passport and boarding pass muttering a flustered "Ek's so jammer."

The skinny man merely grinned before scanning the barcode and handing her passport and ticket stub back to her.

Panting, she repeated in English, "I. Am. So. Sorry," as she raced through the gate.

When she neared the end of the corridor, she realized that she needed to use the restroom, but that she had to wait until she had boarded the plane. The attendants urged her toward the aircraft door.

"Welcome aboard," a young blonde flight attendant, in a dark blue blazer and neckerchief, said. "Mrs. du Plessis, you are in seat 32J." She smiled as she checked the ticket stub before pointing in the direction of Chrisna's seat.

Pushing clumsily through the narrow aisle, Chrisna felt the annoyed stares of the other passengers, and when her purse struck an elderly woman's head, she apologized with a quick 'skees' and continued pushing past the seats, the increasing pressure on her bladder reaching alarming levels.

When she finally located her row of seats, she forced a grin at the large man with the shiny bald head, sitting next to the aisle, in seat 32H.

He grunted, unbuckled the seat belt hidden beneath his potbelly, and squeezed out of his seat. She involuntarily pushed her thighs together as she waited for him to stand, praying that she could hold out until after takeoff.

Sitting down in the middle seat, she placed her purse on her lap and stared at the metal 'G' on the side of the bag while jerking her right leg up and down.

With a few loud groans, the bald man took his seat again, and she shifted as far right as she could manage when he placed his arm over the entire armrest.

"Flight attendants prepare for take-off," came the call from the cockpit.

Fastening her seat belt, Chrisna gripped her purse as the plane started vibrating underneath her.

"You'll have to put your bag underneath the seat in front of you, sweetie."

Chrisna looked at the woman sitting in the window seat. She had to be in her early forties but she looked youthful with her, asymmetrical fiery-red, bob hairstyle. Her daring blue eye shadow would've made a less attractive woman look silly, but it accentuated her vibrant cobalt eyes perfectly. She had three silver studs in her left ear and a blue and silver feather dangling from the right. Her bright red t-shirt, which stretched over a black long sleeved shirt, sported the words, '*You had me at Merlot*', and Chrisna couldn't help but smile.

"Do you need me to help you?" the woman asked in a husky voice.

Shaking her head, Chrisna bent down to place her purse underneath the seat in front of her, but quickly jolted upright again, arching her back when the pressure on her bladder increased.

"Ladies and gentlemen, welcome on board Flight 372BA, with service from London to Paris. We're currently third in line for take-off, and expect to be in the air in approximately ten minutes. Please direct your attention to the monitors as we review the emergency procedures. Thank you and enjoy your flight."

Shifting in her seat, Chrisna clasped her hands together in her lap and jerked her right leg up and down again, faster this time. She stared at the monitor in the back of the seat in front of her as the video stipulated the importance of knowing the location of the closest exit. Glancing to the front and back of the cabin, she made sure that she knew exactly where the closest restroom was.

When the screen went black again, she leaned her head back against her seat, closed her eyes, and bit down on her lower lip, her back still slightly arched to relieve the pressure on her bladder.

"Are you praying?" the woman with the husky voice asked, as though she could sense Chrisna's thoughts.

"No," Chrisna whispered, not opening her eyes.

A few seconds later, she felt a hand on her right knee,

and she opened her eyes.

"Here," the woman said and removed her thin gold-chain necklace, with what looked like a sapphire pendant dangling from it, and held it out to her. "It'll help, trust me. It gives me courage. I think it's lucky."

"Courage?" Chrisna asked confused.

"Yeah. The flying-thing doesn't bother me, but I get that some people can get scared when—"

"I'm not scared of flying," Chrisna said while wishing that the plane would take off so she could run to the restroom.

"You're not?" the woman asked, looking surprised.

Chrisna shook her head and clenched her jaw as she peaked at the blue stone encased in the golden teardrop setting.

The woman grinned. "I love the take-off. It's a rush every time. Boom!"

Chrisna jumped in her seat.

The lights in the cabin dimmed as the taxiing aircraft accelerated and the pressure on her bladder increased with the vibration of the plane.

Lucky? Chrisna thought and grabbed the necklace from her quirky co-passenger. She tightly clutched it in her hand, her knuckles white as bone, and closed her eyes again as the plane took off.

It felt like hours before the captain's voice finally came over the intercom. "Good afternoon, ladies and gentlemen. This is Captain Jarrod Wall speaking. First, I'd like to welcome you on board Flight 372BA, London to Paris. We are currently ascending to an altitude of 33 000 feet and will be cruising at an airspeed of approximately 400 miles per hour. The time now is 2.48pm. The skies are clear and, with the tailwind on our side, we are expecting to land in Paris on time. Estimated flight time is 1 hour and 14 minutes..."

Chrisna slowly opened her eyes as the plane leveled, and she saw that the cabin lights had come back on.

"...The weather in Paris is clear and sunny, with a high of 21 degrees Celsius for this afternoon. And we should be able to get a great view of the city as we descend. The cabin crew will be serving beverages in a few minutes, so please sit back, relax, and enjoy the rest of the flight."

The fasten-your-seat-belt light pinged off and Chrisna quickly unbuckled her seatbelt, pushing herself up. Holding onto the back of the seat in front of her, she crossed her legs and anxiously waited for the grunting bald man to stand up.

Realizing that the necklace was still clutched in her hand, she turned to the red-haired woman, who was now staring out the window. She wanted to return the necklace but her path cleared when the bald man stepped into the aisle, and she sprinted toward the restroom signs near the back of the plane.

Bumping against some of the seats as she tried to keep her balance, she repeated the word '*skees*' all the way to the back.

When she reached the ladies' room, the door closed

in front of her and she glanced back at the other restrooms near the middle of the cabin. The bald man was blocking the aisle, apparently waiting for her return, so she shifted her weight from one foot to the other, breathing in and exhaling slowly while clenching her jaw.

Just as she turned to run to the other restroom, – not caring whether she had to charge through the bald man, the door opened, and the elderly woman she'd struck with her purse earlier shuffled out, giving her a mischievous grin.

Leaping past the elderly woman and into the tiny ladies' room, Chrisna then realized why the woman had grinned as a pungent odor stung her nostrils. Gagging, she realized she had no other option but to do what she came here to do. Holding her breath, she struggled to close the door properly as she did a cross-legged dance. The necklace slipped out of her hand, falling to the floor.

After a few seconds, she gave up on locking the door, drew an involuntary breath, and used the toilet while trying to hold the door shut. The relief relaxed her entire body and she sighed deeply.

When she was done, she finally had the patience and coherence to lock the door properly and pick up the necklace, making sure it wasn't scratched before placing it on the paper towel dispenser.

Washing her hands, she looked at herself in the mirror. Her long, dark brown hair looked tousled and stray strands stood in every direction. Mascara lines darkened the skin underneath her gray eyes and her lip-gloss had long since faded.

In her rush to reach the restroom, she forgot her purse underneath the seat, so she removed her glasses with a shrug, placed them on the sink, and washed her face as best she could before drying her skin with the scratchy paper towel.

Picking up her glasses, she cleaned them on the hem of her buttoned white blouse that stuck out from under her sweater, before returning them to her nose.

Glancing at the mirror a final time, she sighed deeply, and exited the restroom.

As she moved past the bald man again, she noticed the big sweat stains on his oversized blue shirt and smelled his musty body odor.

"I'm Zenelda," the red-haired woman said, stretching out her hand when Chrisna sat down again.

Quickly fastening her seatbelt, she took the woman's hand. "Chrisna."

Smiling broadly, Zenelda shook her hand, almost aggressively. "As in Hare *Krishna*?"

"Skees?"

"What?"

Chrisna's cheeks heated up as she pulled her hand back. "I'm sorry, I keep doing that. I meant to say '*excuse me*'," she said in her thick Afrikaans accent.

"Where are you from?" Zenelda asked.

"Jacobsdal."

"And where's that?"

"Free State…" Chrisna paused. "South Africa. I'm

from a small farm town in South Africa." She rolled her 'R's'.

Zenelda grinned. "I'm very familiar with a place like that. I ran away from a place like that once." She shifted in her seat. "Brattleboro, Vermont, USA," she said, glancing out the window. "Do you like this small farm town of yours?"

"I do," Chrisna said, and then hesitated for a moment. "I guess." She looked down at her hands and a sudden panic rose in her throat. "I will be right back." She unclasped her seat belt and stood up.

Grunting loudly, the bald man pushed himself up and stepped into the aisle once again.

Chrisna rushed toward the restroom but had to stop when a flight attendant pushed a large cart toward her, blocking the aisle. "We're serving drinks. Please use the restrooms near the middle of the cabin."

Glancing past the flight attendant at the restroom where she'd left the necklace, Chrisna sighed, and then turned around, pushed past the bald man, and returned to her seat.

"Are you okay?" Zenelda asked when Chrisna sat down.

"Ja, I'm fine." She fastened her seat belt again.

"I know that feeling. When you gotta go, you gotta go." Zenelda smiled and the tiny wrinkles around her cobalt eyes deepened. "Ooh, that's beautiful."

"Skees?"

"Your wedding ring. I love the setting."

Chrisna looked down at the gold band with the tiny diamond in the rose-shaped setting. "Oh, thank you."

"So, how long have you been married?"

Chrisna twirled her ring around her finger. "I'm divorced." A lump appeared in her throat when she realized what she'd admitted.

Zenelda frowned. "How old are you?"

"Twenty-nine."

"Are you going to Paris for business?"

Chrisna felt uncomfortable with all the questions, and she wasn't sure how much she should tell this strange woman, but before she could answer, Zenelda continued, "I just turned forty-two. I'm on my way to the *Mettre en Valeur* Festival that starts the day after tomorrow. It's gonna be epic. Boom!"

Chrisna jumped in her seat again.

"Two dry red wines, please," Zenelda said, raising her hand in the air as the drinks cart stopped next to their row. "Every year my husband and I take separate trips," she said to Chrisna, who glanced at Zenelda's ring finger with the tiny musical bars tattooed around it. "I call it a marital sabbatical, but Joe just calls it freedom for a week." She reached over Chrisna to take the drinks. "Thanks. It's just one of the things we do to keep our marriage fresh."

"Would you like something to drink?" the flight attendant asked, and Chrisna looked from Zenelda to the flight attendant, and then shook her head before looking back at Zenelda again.

"This year I'm going to Paris," Zenelda said. "To Place de la Concorde. That's where the festival is held. It's the biggest music festival in Europe and they only hold it every five years. This year we're gonna party like it's July."

Chrisna frowned. "But it is July."

"Exactly. No expectations. You should come."

When the flight attendant pushed the cart farther down the aisle, Chrisna unclasped her seat belt and stood up again. "Excuse me."

The bald man frowned and shook his head.

"Please," Chrisna whispered, and watched as he squeezed out of his seat for the fourth time.

She shuddered to think what the other passengers thought as she rushed to the restroom again, sighing with relief when she found the necklace exactly where she'd left it, on the paper towel dispenser.

Walking back to her seat, the plane suddenly dipped, and she stumbled across the aisle. Landing face down on the dark blue carpet, she felt the blood rush to her cheeks.

Crawling to where her glasses had landed a few feet away, she pushed them back onto her nose, and stood up.

The bald man scowled as she shifted past him again.

Flopping down in her seat, she held the necklace out to Zenelda, who gave her a sympathetic look. "No, you keep it for now. I think you need it more than I do," she said and touched Chrisna's arm.

Holding onto the necklace, Chrisna placed her hands in her lap and stared at the sapphire. "I don't think it's working." She sniffed. "I've been in cars, planes, and stuck in airports since yesterday morning. I'm tired and everything keeps going wrong."

"Ah hell, are you crying?" Zenelda inquired, taking Chrisna's chin between her thumb and forefinger, and lifting her face to get a good look at her.

Removing her glasses, Chrisna wiped her eyes with the back of her hand before more tears could escape.

Zenelda pried the necklace from Chrisna's grasp. "Never waste your tears, sweetie," she said as she leaned over and fastened it around Chrisna's neck. "You might really need them one day." She leaned back in her seat. "I believe that there are only three reasons one should ever cry. When you're listening to great music, when you're truly happy, or when someone needs you to cry."

Chrisna frowned. "You don't cry when you're upset?"

"No. I used to, but I haven't done that in forever."

"How is that possible?"

"A long time ago, and I mean a very long time ago, during my high school prom, I locked myself in the ladies' room stall and cried for what seemed like hours. It felt like my world was going to end because my date had kissed some other girl. Then, a couple of girls came in and started talking about some book they've read, called *Risings*. They sounded obsessed with the beautiful main character, Zenelda, and spoke about how strong she was, her spontaneous personality, and her fearlessness."

"Zenelda? Like *your* name?" Chrisna asked.

Zenelda smiled. "Not exactly. I used to be just plain old Anna Feldman." She held out her hand. "Nice to meet you."

Chrisna grinned, replaced her glasses, and shook her hand again. "So what happened?" she asked intrigued.

"No wait, hold the train. Take off your glasses."

Chrisna frowned. "Why?"

"I wanna check something. Please?"

Chrisna removed her glasses and Zenelda stared at her for a long time, making her feel uncomfortable.

"What?"

"For the life of me, I don't understand why you'd wear those."

"What do you mean?"

Zenelda leaned in and frowned as she intensely examined Chrisna's eyes. "You have the most beautiful gray eyes, almost transparent, with little specs of blue in them. You should consider cutting your hair short. It'll make your eyes pop."

Chrisna cleared her throat. "Thank you," she said, feeling uneasy, and quickly placed her glasses back onto her nose.

"Do you *have* to wear them?"

Fidgeting with the end of her ponytail, Chrisna asked, "So what happened next in the ladies' room at your prom?"

"Well, I stayed quiet and listened as those girls rambled on about this outgoing, adventurous, free-spirited, wild, seductive woman, called Zenelda. When they left, I stepped out of the stall, looked at myself in the mirror, wiped my eyes, and said, '*You* could be a Zenelda.' I bought the book the very next day and became Zenelda from then on. I left that small town behind when I turned eighteen and never looked back. When I got to LA, I met the lead singer of a rock band and toured the country with them. Eventually, I started touring with other bands and even traveled overseas to the most wonderful places."

Chrisna frowned. "Are you still in a band?"

"Aw, sweetie, no. I never was *in* a band. I took care of the band's wardrobe and…um, social life."

Chrisna raised her eyebrows. "You're a groupie?"

"Was." Zenelda smiled. "And I prefer the term *Music Aficionado*." The wrinkles around her eyes deepened again. "I got married almost fifteen years ago to Joe, Joe Gentry." Zenelda looked at Chrisna as if she was supposed to know who Joe was, but when Chrisna didn't respond, she continued, "He's a well-known songwriter, and now I own my own record store in London. I actually met my husband at the same festival I'm going to now."

The plane dipped for a second time and Chrisna quickly fastened her seatbelt moments before the fasten-seat-belt sign pinged on again.

"Ladies and gentlemen, we are experiencing some turbulence. Please return to your seats."

"So, what do *you* do?" Zenelda inquired.

"I'm a teacher at Jacobsdal Landbouskool," she said. "I teach Afrikaans."

"So why *are* you going to Paris?"

"It was my best friend's stupid idea." She clenched her jaw when the plane shook violently for a few seconds. "A birthday present. Five days in Paris."

"That's an amazing present. When's your birthday?"

The cabin stopped shaking. "Sunday."

"Wow, happy birthday."

"Thanks."

"Celebrating the big 3-0 in Paris, how wonderful." Zenelda mused.

"I guess." Chrisna relented as she fidgeted with the sapphire. "About two months ago, Sandra and I were watching the Sunday night movie. There was a scene on the Eiffel Tower, so I joked and said that I wouldn't have breakfast on it, but that I would love to throw my wedding ring off the top. So here I am."

"Really?"

"Ja. Silly, I know. Anyway, Sandra raised money from friends, family, and even from the people I work with, and gave me a voucher for this trip. She said it was a 'divorce present'. It's the school holidays now, so...I guess she thought she was being funny when she gave me the card, because she wrote '*Gooi hom, kwagga*' in it."

Zenelda frowned.

"It literally means, *throw it, zebra*. It's an Afrikaans thing. I can't really explain it."

"Boom!" Zenelda said, and Chrisna shuddered before chuckling softly.

"Why do you keep doing that?"

"What?"

"Say *Boom!*?"

The bald man shushed her, and Zenelda glared at him. "Really?" she said, glowering at him before turning back to face Chrisna. "*Boom* is like a better way to express surprise. It's a Zenelda thing. I can't really explain it."

Chrisna unintentionally giggled and then quickly stopped herself.

"So, your plan is to go to Paris and throw that gorgeous ring off the top of the Eiffel Tower?"

Chrisna looked at her wedding ring. "I don't know."

"I think it's an awesome idea. I support it one hundred percent."

"You do?"

"Yeah, never be afraid to be afraid of what you're afraid of. Embrace the fear, and release the crazy."

Chrisna arched her eyebrows and stared at her.

"Think about it," Zenelda said and stretched her back. "How long have you been divorced?"

"One month and twelve days."

Zenelda frowned. "Then why are you still wearing your wedding ring?"

"I don't know. I guess I feel naked without it."

"One should never be afraid to feel naked. But you're not still in love with him, are you?"

Feeling her chest tightening, Chrisna took a deep breath. "No, it's over."

"Do you have kids?"

"No."

"Me neither," Zenelda said. "So, what *are* your plans exactly?"

Twirling her ring around her finger again, she sighed. "To forget about him."

Zenelda cleared her throat. "I meant while you're in Paris."

Chrisna straightened her posture and looked up. "Well, I bought this amazing guidebook to all the must-see sights in Paris." Bending down, she opened her purse and pulled out a paperback with the words *Must-See Sights in Paris* printed on the front. As she held it up, Zenelda glanced at the cover with the various photographs of the Eiffel Tower, Notre Dame, and the Sacre Coeur on it.

Chrisna flipped thoughtfully through the yellow-highlighted pages. "I have a whole itinerary planned down to the last minute, so I don't miss a thing." She stopped on one of the pages and pointed at a photograph. "Tomorrow I will visit the Louvre. If I get up at six-forty I can be out of the hotel by seven-forty, grab a coffee and croissant, and be at the museum by eight. Since my hotel is very close to the Louvre, I can walk. I love to walk. And then in the afternoon—"

"Stop the boat." Zenelda threw her hands up.

"What?"

Smiling, Zenelda reached down and picked up Chrisna's purse. "I bet you have a French phrase book in here as well." She opened the bag.

"You can't just—"

"Boom!" Zenelda pulled out a small book with the title *French Phrases You Can't Do Without*.

"Is jy mal? What are you doing?" Chrisna asked and grabbed the book, pushing it back into her purse. Taking the purse from Zenelda, she put the guidebook away as well and shoved the bag back in underneath the seat in front of her.

With her arms folded, Zenelda frowned at Chrisna. "Your itinerary is a bad idea. That's no way to experience the wonders of Paris." She sat up straight. "Do you have a pen and paper in that magic bag of yours?"

She hesitantly said, "Ja."

"Please hand them to me and I'll write down the only five things you have to do while you're in Paris."

Intrigued, Chrisna took a pen and a small notepad from her purse and handed it to her.

After a few seconds of scribbling, Zenelda handed the pad back to her, and Chrisna struggled to read the almost illegible writing.

"Go ahead. Read it out loud."

Clearing her throat and shifting in her seat, she started reading. "One. *Hug the Venus de Milo.*" She frowned at Zenelda.

"That's a fun one, but you have to be very quick, *and* able to disappear in a crowd."

"Two. *Get a mime to speak.* Seriously?" She glanced up at Zenelda.

"It's not impossible."

"Three. *Sing in front of a crowd of at least fifty people.*" She looked up again. "Never going to happen."

"That's the easiest one!" Zenelda exclaimed.

"Four. *Dance the Tango in the rain in front of the Notre Dame.*"

Zenelda smiled. "I love that one but the weather does play a big part."

"Five. *Make passionate love to a Parisian.*" Chrisna gaped at her, eyes opening and closing as though she were looking at a crazy person. Perhaps she was…

"Bonjour," the bald man said, and Zenelda burst out in a high-pitched laugh.

Ripping the piece of paper from her notepad, she handed it to Zenelda. "You're very creative but you can keep your list."

Folding the paper into a tiny square, Zenelda bent down and pushed it into the side pocket of Chrisna's purse. "You never know."

"Ladies and gentlemen, we have begun our descent. Please make sure your seats are in the upright position and tray tables are stowed away. All items should be in the overhead compartments or underneath the seat in front of you. We hope you enjoyed your flight with us…"

Zenelda leaned back in her seat. "I was serious when I asked you to come to the festival with me."

"Thank you," Chrisna said. "But I don't think—"

"I'll be waiting under the Arch de Triomphe at one o' clock on Friday." Zenelda looked out the window as the city of Paris appeared underneath them.

When the plane came to a halt and the fasten-seat-belt sign pinged off, Chrisna unclasped her seatbelt, stood up, and waited for the bald man to retrieve his carry-on from the overhead compartment.

Taking her purse from underneath the seat, Chrisna stepped into the aisle and made space for Zenelda to pass.

Zenelda took a small suitcase from the overhead compartment and turned to Chrisna. "You have a nice trip now, Kristal."

She frowned. "It's Chrisna."

"I know, but *you* could be a Kristal." Zenelda grinned and set off down the aisle.

Chrisna looked down and saw the teardrop pendant around her neck. "Wait! Your necklace!" she called, struggling to unclasp the chain.

There were already four people between them when Zenelda looked back. "You can give it to me when you come to the festival on Friday. Remember, under the Arc de Triomphe at one. Don't lose it now. It's a family heirloom."

Chrisna tried to push past the people to catch up to Zenelda, but she disappeared into the crowd.

Two

Chrisna woke slowly.

Pushing against the rough material of the armrest, she sat up on the single brown couch. Her head throbbed, and for a moment, she couldn't remember where she was.

As she tried to force her eyes to adjust to the harsh light streaming in from the window, she realized that she wasn't wearing her glasses and she peered through her heavy eyelids at the small, blurry room. Two single beds with white covers and brown throw pillows stood pushed together against the opposite beige wall, and took up half the space in the room. Neither one of the beds appeared to have been slept in, and next to her, a small wooden desk stood underneath a wall mounted flat screen television.

It was her hotel room, she realized with relief.

Standing up, she suddenly felt lightheaded and steadied herself against the couch before walking to the nightstand. She would always leave her glasses on it before going to bed, but they weren't there. Finding her cell phone on the desk near the metallic lamp, she saw that the battery had died, and then she took her charger and the adapter plug out of the desk drawer, plugging it into the odd-looking socket.

She noticed her purse on the chair by the desk and opened a small compartment on the side of her bag, pulled out a white paper sachet, and walked into the tiny bathroom.

She stopped when her bare feet touched the cold white tiles and looked down at her clothes. The bottom three buttons of her now much wrinkled blue, long-sleeved blouse were undone, and there was a white chalk stain on the left knee of her black pants.

Reaching the sink, she stared at her blurred reflection in the mirror. Her hair was untied and she looked a mess with mascara streaks running down her cheeks.

Tearing the sachet open, she sprinkled the bitter white headache powder on her tongue, opened the small bottle of water, which stood on the sink, and washed the powder down. Still thirsty, she gulped down the rest of the water.

She closed the bathroom door, brushed her teeth and undressed, before placing Zenelda's necklace, her wedding ring and watch on the sink.

Taking a shower, she let the warm spray splash over her face and pictured the previous day's events. She remembered the busy Charles de Gaulle Airport where she had picked up her luggage. Zenelda was nowhere to be found. She recalled the pale man with the pencil mustache; it took him over an hour to drive her to her hotel in his small silver taxicab. She remembered unpacking her luggage when she had finally made it to her room, after the lengthy check-in. She'd messaged Sandra and her parents, letting them know that she had safely arrived in Paris. She knew she had dressed in her blue blouse, black pants, and black pumps before setting off for dinner at a nearby restaurant. After that, her mind was a complete blank.

Stepping out of the shower, she rolled her long hair into a towel before drying herself off and putting on the fluffy hotel robe.

Placing the dirty clothes into one of several black bags she had neatly stacked on one of the closet shelves, she shoved the bag into the empty compartment below the bottom shelf. She searched for the black pumps she had worn with the outfit, but couldn't find them anywhere. She looked under the bed but her shoes were gone. Where were her shoes?

Standing up, she closed the striped curtains and walked to the closet. She took out a gray short-sleeved blouse with a pink floral pattern lining both sides of the buttons, blue jeans, white socks, and white trainers, and dressed.

She opened the curtains again, and light spilled into the room, as she reached into her purse, glad that she brought along the extra pair of glasses with the bright blue-rim.

As she returned the casing to her purse, Chrisna spotted an unfamiliar silver coin protruding from between the pages of her notepad. It was about the size of a One-Euro piece with an engraving of an eight-point star on the one side, and on the other side it had three small flowers that looked like daisies.

Having no idea how the coin had ended up in her bag, she searched through all the compartments and found the folded piece of paper with the only-things-worth-doing-in-Paris list that Zenelda had shoved in her purse. Could she have sneaked the coin in there as well? Why would she do that?

She pushed the piece of paper and the coin into a small compartment inside her purse and shrugged as she zipped it closed.

By the time she had dried her hair and noticed the time, it was already, 1.35pm. Her heart skipped a beat.

She put her wedding ring back on and lifted the sapphire pendant from the sink to look at it again. It was beautiful and probably worth a lot of money - not something one would leave in a hotel room. She fastened the necklace around her neck and rushed back into the bedroom to turn on the cell phone, which was charging on the nightstand.

The fact that she had forgotten to set her alarm the night before puzzled her, but she shrugged off the thought, and scrolled to the Itinerary App., and read her scheduled events for the day.

8am: Visit the Louvre.

11.45am: Musée Delacroix.

1.45pm: Lunch in the Tuileries Gardens & Sightseeing.

3.50pm: Orangerie Museum.

5.15pm: Musée d'Orsay.

7.15pm: Dinner.

8.45pm: Walk along the Seine River.

She took a deep breath, pressed the edit button on the App. and adjusted the times to the scheduled events to compensate for running late. The walk along the Seine River would start at 9.45pm, and Chrisna hoped that she would not be too jet-lagged to enjoy it at that time of the night. She also hadn't left herself much time to really appreciate any of the activities schedules for the day, but it would just have to do.

Saving the new entries, she unplugged her phone, shoved it into her purse before removing her glasses and heading to the bathroom. She leaned close to the mirror to apply a quick layer of moisturizer, mascara and lip-gloss before replacing her spectacles, grabbing her purse and rushing out of the room.

Chrisna smiled as she stepped out of the hotel's cool, air-conditioned lobby into the fresh outdoors. As the school's hockey coach, she was fit and ready for all the walking that would take place today. Being free to move around was a great step up from being stuck on different modes of transport for days. She fell into a brisk step as she walked down the sidewalk of Rue Croix-des-Petits-Champs, in the direction of The Louvre, still puzzled by the disappearance of her glasses and shoes.

"Kristal!" she heard someone call, but she did not recognize her new name, bestowed on her by the mysterious Zenelda. Suddenly, she heard hurried footsteps catching up to her, and as she turned to look, the man grabbed her arm and came to a halt in front of her and stopped, blocking her way. "Kristal! Wow, you're fast," he said, looking directly at her with a curious half-smile on his ruggedly attractive face.

He was tall, with almost-black hair that covered his ears and almost touched his shoulders. He wore blue jeans, leather sandals, a white t-shirt, and the strap of a bright blue backpack stretched from his side across his chest. He couldn't have been older than thirty-five.

Chrisna smiled politely as she stepped around him, and continued down the sidewalk.

"Kristal!" he called again. "I have your shoes."

She stopped and turned around as her heart dropped to her stomach. What does this stranger know about her shoes? Her eyes narrowed suspiciously, her hands forming involuntary fists.

Reaching into his backpack, he pulled out a pair of black pumps and held them up.

Mesmerized, Chrisna walked back toward him, – stopping a few feet away, gaping at the shoes, then at the man. "Those are mine?" she asked surprised, but she already knew the answer from the small scuff mark on the left heel.

Trepidation filled her as he took a step forward and

smiled broadly, his bright olive-green eyes almost shimmered in the sunlight. His eyes were hypnotic. The bright green irises were encircled by black, and although the whites seemed slightly pink – maybe he was tired – it contrasted the thick lashes that were almost too pretty for a guy. "You were very persistent about getting them back," he said, and Chrisna detected a British accent.

"I was?" she asked, glancing from him to the shoes and back to him again.

His smile touched his eyes. "Adamant might be a better word."

"I'm sorry, who are you? And why do you have my shoes?"

A frown replaced his smile. "Tyce."

"Tyce?"

He looked disappointed for a second before he smiled again. "Tyce Turcotte. Come on, Kristal, you're kidding, right?"

"Why do you keep calling me Kristal?"

"Well, that's your name, isn't it? Do you want me to call you something else?"

Then Chrisna remembered that *Kristal* was the name Zenelda had called her before they'd left the plane. "I told you my name was Kristal?"

"Yes," he said and frowned again.

"Why do you have my shoes?" she asked, a little afraid of the answer.

He grinned. "You don't remember?"

Fidgeting with the end of her ponytail, she shook her

head.

"Wow, bummer. We had such a great time."

Embarrassed that she couldn't remember what had happened after she'd left the hotel room the previous night, she asked, "Did we...?" Blushing, she looked down at the thin blue stripes on her trainers. "You know...did we...?"

When she looked up again, he smiled broadly. "If you mean, have fun. Yes we did." He shook his head. "Otherwise, no," he said with a disappointed sideway pout.

She sighed with relief. "Skees, I can't remember anything after I left the hotel room to have dinner last night."

An image of a restaurant popped into her head. She saw small wooden tables with pink linen standing outfront. Maroon patio umbrellas stood in between every second row of tables, behind large concrete pillars that connected three archways. Yellow ambient lighting shone through the large glass windows, separating the inside from the outside dining area.

"Wait, I remember the restaurant! I had some kind of chicken with onions, bacon, and carrots."

"Coq au Vin."

"Skees?"

He smiled. "The dish is called *Coq au Vin*."

She frowned. "Oh, right, and I had a glass of wine. I don't usually drink." She thought for a second. "No, two, I had two glasses of red wine." She strained her mind to remember more but couldn't. "That's it. That's all I remember."

"Come on," Tyce said and pushed her shoes back into his backpack. "I'll buy you a cup of coffee and tell you how I ended up with your shoes."

She glanced at her watch, and then in the direction she was heading.

"We can go there." Tyce pointed to a small building with a red and white awning, and a few wooden tables and chairs standing on the outside.

Chrisna sighed, thinking about her planned sightseeing, but she was dying for a cup of coffee, too. "I don't know—"

"Oh, come on," he said, grabbing her hand and pulling her toward the nearest table.

She tried to object, but before she could utter a word, they had reached the café.

"Have a seat, I'll get the coffee," Tyce said as he let go of her hand, placing his backpack on one of the chairs and walking into the quaint café.

Chrisna sat down resolutely, holding her purse on her lap as she shifted uncomfortably in her seat. She glanced at the menu on the chalkboard that stood a few feet away. 'Café Crème, Café Allongé, Café Noisette'.

"Je peux avoir une cigarette?"

She looked up to see a bony man with messy gray hair and tanned skin that looked like rubber. Deep wrinkles covered most of his face.

"Je peux avoir une cigarette?" he said again, sounding

a little angry as he stepped closer and leaned over the table. He smelled like hot garbage.

"Skees. Ek praat nie Frans nie," Chrisna said, shifting her chair back, tightly gripping her purse, and turning her head away.

"Je peux avoir une cigarette?" the man said for the third time.

Ready to get up and leave, she saw Tyce walking in her direction. "Désolé, nous pas fumer," he said loudly, and the man shuffled off, mumbling something as he left.

"Thank you," Chrisna said when Tyce sat down next to her. "What did he want?"

"A cigarette. I told him we don't smoke. What did *you* tell him?"

"I tried to tell him that I don't speak French."

"*Je ne parle pas Français,*" Tyce said.

Chrisna tried to copy his pronunciation but failed miserably, and she felt her cheeks heat up as Tyce laughed good-naturedly. He had a warm laugh. She liked his laugh.

"Can't I just say *No French*?"

Placing her purse on the ground underneath the table, she lifted the leg of her chair over the strap, just as the waiter placed two tiny cups of coffee on the table.

Noticing the small cookie on the saucer, her stomach rumbled, as she remembered that she never got around to her croissant before she left the hotel. She quickly placed the cookie in her mouth.

"Are you hungry?" Tyce asked with a smile as he leisurely dipped his cookie into his coffee.

"No," she mumbled, covering her mouth with her hand as she continued to chew. She took a quick sip of her scalding hot coffee to wash down the cookie and pulled a pained face.

"You don't like it?" he asked, taking another small bite of his cookie.

She swallowed. "No, it's just hot. So how did *you* end up with my shoes?"

He smiled again, and she noticed his perfectly straight white teeth. "You left them on the boat."

"Boat?"

"Yes. Boat."

"I was on a boat last night?"

He took a sip of his coffee. "*We* were."

She forced a grin. "I'm going to need a little more information than that."

He sat back in his chair, stretched his arms over his head, before placing his elbows on the table, and twirling the small cup on the saucer. "Well, I met you at *La Fosse*. It's a small music-bar not far from here."

"A music-bar?"

"It's actually a funny story. I haven't been to that bar in a long time, but last night I played a few acoustic songs there because the owner asked me to."

"You're a musician?" she asked intrigued.

"Sometimes." He rubbed the back of his neck before taking another sip of his coffee. "After my set, I went outside to get some air, and you bumped into me."

She listened attentively while blowing on her coffee before taking another sip.

"You asked me for directions to your hotel," he continued, "but you couldn't remember the name."

"Why didn't I just check my phone? All the information of the hotel is on my phone."

"Yeah, we discovered that later, much later. You were upset, and when I couldn't help you, you tried to leave and collided with the message board that stood outside the bar."

"A message board?"

"Yes," he said, "almost exactly like that one." He pointed to the chalkboard with the café's menu on it.

"So that explains the white chalk stain on my pants," she thought aloud.

He smiled again. She definitely liked his smile.

"I invited you inside," he said, "and bought you a drink to try to calm you down."

"What did I drink?" she asked a little worried.

"You insisted on having what I was having," he continued, with an amused glint in his eyes.

"Which was..?"

"Cognac." The smile lines deepened.

She pulled a face. "Really? I drank Cognac?"

"Well, now that I know you had two glasses of wine before that, and taking into account that you'd been travelling, the memory-thing kind of makes sense."

"I told you that?" She took another sip of her coffee.

"That I'd been travelling?"

He grinned and rubbed the back of his neck again. "You kind of told me a little more than that."

"Like what?" She feared his answer.

"I know about your wedding ring mission."

She looked at her hands and twirled her ring around her finger.

"I'm sorry," he said and leaned forward, touching her hand almost imperceptibly. But she pulled back immediately, placing her hands in her lap. He sat back in his chair. "Don't worry, I'm pretty forgetful too." He bumped his forehead with the palm of his hand. "Already forgotten, wiped from my mind, gone, vanished, passé." Shooting his fingers in the air, he gestured an explosion. "Poof!"

She smiled. "How did we end up on the boat?"

"I was invited to a friend's birthday party, and intended to go there after my set at the bar. The party was on the boat."

"So you took me with you?"

"Not right away," he said. "We talked for a while, and I asked if there was anyone I could call, but you said that anyone worth calling was already asleep, and you didn't want to bother them. Oh, and we had another drink—"

"I had two glasses of cognac? No wonder I can't remember." Her stomach rumbled loudly.

"You *are* hungry," he said and waved the waiter over. "Deux croissants au beurre, s'il vous plait."

Chrisna frowned.

"Don't worry, its food, I promise." He took the last sip of his coffee. "We left the bar just before eleven. I walked around with you to see if you recognized any of the streets but, of course, you didn't."

She pushed her glasses up on her nose. "Of course."

"We walked around for about an hour…"

The waiter returned with two croissants on separate plates.

"Merci," Tyce said in a perfect French accent.

Chrisna repeated the word, rolling her 'R'.

Picking up one of the croissants, he took a bite, and then gestured to her to do the same. Starving, she didn't hesitate to take a big bite.

"Good, right?" he asked.

She nodded and chewed on the piece of warm buttery pastry. "And then what happened?" she mumbled, holding her hand in front of her mouth again.

"You insisted that you wanted to come with me to the party," he said. "And I didn't want you to wander the streets alone." He took another bite of his croissant.

"And the shoes?"

He quickly chewed and then swallowed. "You complained that your feet were killing you after all the walking, and the dancing—"

"I don't dance," she said, almost choking on the pastry.

He chuckled. "Then you fake it very well."

She felt her cheeks heat up again and thought about

the last time she'd danced in public. It was at her wedding reception, eight years ago, but there weren't many opportunities since then. Werner, didn't dance.

"Are you okay?" Tyce interrupted her thoughts.

"So, I took off my shoes on the boat?" she asked and took another bite.

"Yes, you kicked them into the corner and then yelled something like, *Shoes should be banned! Everyone, take off your shoes!*" He had a wide grin on his face. "The funny thing is that everyone did. It was awesome. Everyone loved you. I can't believe you don't remember any of it."

She covered her eyes with her hand. "I can't believe I did that." Lowering her hand, she looked at him. "Anything else I need to be embarrassed about?"

He smiled his perfect smile. "You really shouldn't feel embarrassed. You owned that party. See for yourself."

"What?"

"The evidence is on your phone."

Chrisna hesitated for a moment and then reached into her purse, pulling out her cell phone.

"You demanded that we take plenty photos," he said.

Unlocking her phone, she pressed the gallery button and scrolled through the photographs. The first few were of her with her luggage at Bram Fischer International Airport, in Bloemfontein. Sandra had taken them when she'd dropped her off, insisting that she captured as much as possible of her trip. The next one was of a long white yacht with hundreds of fairy lights and a crowd of people on the top deck.

She scrolled to the next photo and saw herself, arms up in the air, standing on the ramp leading to the entrance of the boat. Scrolling again, she saw several photos of her posing next to men wearing tuxedos and top hats, and women with short fringe dresses and feathers in their hair. She looked up and gaped at Tyce.

"Did I mention it was a Twenties theme-party?"

She held the phone up so he could see the photo. "And you let me go with you dressed like *that*?"

"Keep scrolling," he instructed, cocking a finger at the phone.

She turned the phone back to her, scrolled past more photos of her posing with the guests, and then stopped. Standing next to the rail, she posed with one hand on her hip and the other holding onto the rim of a black top hat. The bottom three buttons of her blue blouse were undone and tied into a knot, exposing her belly button. Too mortified to look at Tyce, she continued scrolling. There were a few photos of him in a black suit, white shirt, and black bowtie, making faces at the camera.

The phone display dimmed and a connect-to-charger message popped up. She stroked her finger over the screen again, and then saw herself leaning over the rail, stretching her arm out, holding onto her black-rim glasses.

She turned the phone so Tyce could see the photo. He laughed his warm laugh. "Yip, you threw them overboard," he said. "I'm not exactly sure why you did that."

"Probably because I'd lost my mind."

"You were a lot of fun." He smiled. "We left the party around four-thirty this morning with a woman you befriended. Her driver was the one who insisted we check your phone for the hotel information."

"So we left barefoot?"

"I had my shoes on again but we couldn't find yours," he said. "When we stopped at your hotel, you were exhausted. So I helped you to your room."

She frowned. "You helped me?"

"Okay, I carried you. But when we reached your room, you demanded that I go back and get your shoes."

"Skees," she said softly, feeling embarrassed.

"I had some errands to run this morning but I was able to go back there just before I came here. I must say, there were still a lot of shoes left on that boat."

She looked at her phone but the connect-to-charger message popped up again, and then the phone went dead so she returned it to her purse. She pulled out the strange silver coin and held it out to him, asking, "Do you know what this is?"

He took the coin from her and examined it. "A coin?"

"So you don't know how I got it?"

"No, I don't, sorry."

She sighed, took the coin from him, and returned it to her purse. "Well, at least now I know most of what happened last night. Thank you."

"I should thank *you*," he said. "I had a blast."

"No really, thanks for my shoes and the coffee and the—"

"Don't mention it."

She placed the last piece of croissant in her mouth, and watched as Tyce looked at his watch while waving the waiter over again, and paying him. "I have to be somewhere but I'll be in Paris for another week or so. Can I see you again?"

She knew she was blushing again and she looked down at her hands. Shifting uncomfortably in her seat, she twirled her ring around her finger. "I don't think so," she said nervously. "I have a lot to do before I go back home. My itinerary is very full." As she said the words, she knew she was making excuses. She was scared.

"I understand," he said, and when she looked up again, she thought he looked disappointed. He stood up and held his hand out to her. She trembled when she took his hand and shook it. "It was fun, Kristal," he said and walked away.

She sat frozen in her seat for a second, and then she spun around. "Tyce!"

He turned around with a grin on his face. "Yes?"

"My shoes…"

Three

Shifting forward, inch by inch, to see the Mona Lisa up close, several tourists pushed against Chrisna to get to the front.

Just over two hours had passed since she'd pushed her pumps into her purse, left the café, and hurried to the Louvre.

And now she was flipping through the brochure she had picked up from the information desk, and reread the facts on the Mona Lisa twice more before she lost track again and had to start over. For some reason she couldn't stop thinking about Tyce and what he'd told her.

When she finally reached the front, an elderly man shoved a camera in her hand. "Photo, photo," he said before posing in front of the painting with an exaggerated smile on his face.

Chrisna took the photo and handed the camera back to him. She stared at the woman in the painting behind the glass casing for a long time and couldn't figure out why she wasn't more impressed. It was beautiful, surely, but a feeling of disappointment lingered in her chest.

Reaching into her purse, she took out her phone to

take a photo but then remember that her battery had died. So she pushed her phone back into her bag, left the crowd, and wandered through the adjacent area.

Eventually, all the paintings started to look the same to her. Rows and rows of priceless artwork and she couldn't force herself to care. The constant hum of voices resonating through the enormous room agitated her as she watched the people sitting on the benches, admiring the artwork.

She stopped next to an artist replicating a massive painting of ascending clouds with various biblical figures on them. She read the nameplate next to the painting; *Coronation of the Virgin – Tintoretto (Venice, c. 1518 – Venice, 1594)*, and then compared the original to the copy. It appeared exactly the same.

Then a phrase popped into her head, '*You fake it very well*', and her throat tightened as her mind flashed on an image of Tyce and his perfect smile.

She shook off the thought and walked away, taking the escalator to the ground floor.

A massive corridor contained a display of Roman antiquities, and Chrisna glanced at the sculptures, busts, and vases.

A young boy ran past her, his sandals slapping on the floor.

She recalled how she didn't think Tyce looked terrible in his sandals and jeans. Sandra would often make fun of the dads who'd show up to parent-teacher nights dressed like that.

Why couldn't she get Tyce out of her head?

An announcement came over the intercom, "Mesdames et Messieurs, le musée fermera en vingt quinze minutes. Ladies and gentlemen, the museum will close in fifteen minutes..." The announcement continued in several other languages and Chrisna sighed.

She pushed the brochure into her purse and briskly walked down the corridor, with the large pillars and archways, to the Greek Antiquities display.

Tyce, Tyce, Tyce. She stopped, closed her eyes, and took a deep breath to get rid of the tightening feeling in her chest. It wasn't a feeling of disappointment like before, it was regret. She regretted not saying yes to him, missing her chance. Exhaling slowly, she cursed herself for being such a coward.

She opened her eyes again, looking up, and a marble sculpture of a woman with no arms towered over her. Her heart skipped a beat and she stood frozen for a few seconds, staring at the statue.

Reaching into her purse, she opened the small compartment and pulled out the folded piece of paper Zenelda had given her. She read the first line, '*Hug the Venus de Milo.*'

She couldn't actually do it, could she? She looked around at the people hurriedly leaving the room, but as most left, more entered. A female security guard, dressed in a black pants suit, stood at the far end of the room, directing the hordes of people toward an exit.

No, she couldn't. That wasn't who she was. She

wasn't the person Tyce had described. She wasn't Kristal.

Pushing the list back into her bag, she walked away.

"I know they're closing, dear," a man said loudly and Chrisna turned around. The man was taking photos of the sculpture while a woman tried to pull him away. "But we'll probably never get this chance again."

Chrisna forcefully blew the air out of her lungs before taking a deep breath and gripping the sapphire pendant in her hand.

Quickly stepping over the low railing, she climbed onto the square pedestal on which the Venus de Milo stood. A few of the onlookers pointed and commented, but Chrisna wrapped her arms around the sculpture's waist for a second, squeezed, and then let go before jumping over the railing again, sliding as she hit the floor.

Running as fast as she could, she reached a large tour group and stepped into the middle of the crowd, crouching down, pretending to talk to an elderly woman, who merely smiled and nodded. Her heart raced and she held her breath as they passed by the security guard. When nothing happened, a huge grin broke out on her face and she felt liberated.

Chrisna tried to catch her breath as she flung her purse onto the couch and flopped down onto the bed.

As soon as she had exited the Louvre, she'd run all the way back to her hotel room.

She glanced at her watch, 6.23pm. Her body tingled and she couldn't remember ever feeling so exhilarated. Perhaps she didn't get everything on her itinerary done, but she got to meet Tyce and she hugged Venus. That was good.

She stood up and pulled her pumps out of her purse, smiled at them for a moment, before placing them on the floor. She kicked off her trainers and took her cell phone out. She plugged it into the charger and turned it on, anxiously waiting for it to start up.

When it finally did, she clicked on the Itinerary App., deleted the entries underneath '*Visit the Louvre*', and in capital letters tapped in, '*HUG THE VENUS DE MILO*'.

She smiled, looked at her wedding ring for a long time, and then beneath that entry she typed, '*Throw wedding ring off the Eiffel Tower*'.

When her phone reached one bar of battery, she tossed it into her purse again, and rushed out the door.

It had taken less than half an hour to reach the Eiffel Tower and she'd smiled the whole way there.

Stepping off the white bus with the turquoise stripe over the windows, she looked up at the massive steel structure towering over her, and she couldn't contain her excitement. She ran the rest of the way but stopped when she saw the multitude of visitors standing underneath the tower.

Not allowing herself to feel discouraged, she walked to the end of the shortest line and looked at her watch. It read 7.45pm, and she was amazed that it was still light out. Back home it would've been pitch black by now.

She looked up and gaped at the massive metal trusses holding the gigantic structure together. Her stomach turned and she felt lightheaded as she watched the moving clouds through the beams.

"Well, hi there," someone said, and she looked behind her.

A plump middle-aged woman with short ash-blonde hair was smiling at her. She wore a denim jacket that covered most of The Stars and Stripes on her t-shirt, and a skin-colored travel pouch stuck out from underneath the hem.

"Hi, how are you?" Chrisna asked and smiled politely.

"You ain't from the States," the woman said in a high-pitched voice. "Where you from? No, wait, lemme guess. I ain't bad at this. Say somethin' else."

Chrisna frowned. "What do you want me to say?"

"Australia!" the woman exclaimed enthusiastically.

"Australia," Chrisna repeated.

"Wow! I was right." The woman looked surprised. "You're from Australia!"

"Oh, no. No, I'm not from Australia," Chrisna said, suddenly realizing what had happened. "Skees."

The woman looked disappointed. "Then say somethin' else."

Chrisna thought for a second. "Ek is ook nie 'n Hollander nie."

"Dutch!" the women cried out and turned to a much older man standing off to the side. "Jed. This lady's from Holland."

The gray-haired, chubby man forced a grin. He also wore an American flag t-shirt but his stretched over his protruding stomach. He carried a large backpack and a white bag in each hand.

"That's Jed, my husband. He ain't much of a talker. I'm Augusta. We're from Little Rock, Arkansas."

"Hi," she said and shook the woman's hand. "I'm Chrisna, but I'm not from Holland. I'm from South Africa."

"Really?" Augusta's eyes widened.

The line moved and Chrisna took two steps forward.

"What's Africa like?" Augusta asked.

Chrisna frowned and thought about the strange question for a second. "*South* Africa is beautiful." She didn't know how else to answer. "But I've never been to other African countries."

Augusta looked confused. "Say somethin' in *South* African again."

Struggling to hide her amusement, Chrisna said, "We have eleven official languages. There's Sotho, Zulu, Xhosa..." She tried to make the click sound with her tongue but failed. "Venda, Ndebele, English, Afrikaans..." She wracked her brain for the ones she'd missed but it didn't look like Augusta had noticed.

"Woo-e, that's a lot," Augusta said. "How long you been here for?"

"Since yesterday."

"We've been here for a week." She pointed to her husband, who wasn't paying any attention to his wife. "We're fixin' to leave on Monday."

"Did you have a nice trip?"

"Yeah, we were at the Bastille, the Sacre Coeur, the Louvre..."

Chrisna grinned when she recalled hugging the Venus de Milo.

Augusta continued, "The Notre Dame, that big graveyard..." She turned to her husband. "Jed, gimme the camera."

The chubby man sighed, put the bags down, opened his backpack, and handed his wife a small digital camera.

Augusta switched it on and held it out so Chrisna could see the screen. "This is where we ate the first night." She pointed to a blurry photo of Jed looking annoyed as he sat on the opposite side of a dimly lit table. "The food was lovely." Augusta continued scrolling through dozens of photos of her and her husband at the various tourist sights she'd mentioned. Jed didn't smile in any of the photos.

"This was taken at the Sacre Coeur," Augusta continued, pointing to a photograph of a man hanging from the top of a tall lamppost with a blue sky in the background. "That man hung there for a long time and bounced a soccer ball on his foot."

The line moved again and Chrisna quickly shuffled forward as Augusta continued clicking the button on the camera.

"Is this your first time in Paris?" Chrisna asked, hoping to distract the woman before she could show her anymore photos.

"Bless your heart, no. We've been here before. The first time was in 1984…"

Chrisna glanced at Jed, who was holding up three fingers behind his wife's back. She smiled at the poor man and, for a second, she thought she saw his mouth pull into a slight grin, but then he looked annoyed again.

The long line of people still ahead of her took another step forward.

"We weren't gonna go up again this year but Jed wanted to climb the stairs." Augusta pointed at part of the tower above the ticket office, and Chrisna saw Jed shaking his head. "We've been to Italy, Greece and Holland," Augusta continued. "Maybe we should go to South Africa next." She glanced at her husband. "I've always wanted to go on a safari."

"You should," a broad shouldered man, standing behind Jed, said.

Augusta turned around. "Have you been?"

"We went on a safari last year," the man said, pointing to a short black-haired woman next to him. "The Kruger National Park is beautiful. We saw three of the Big Five in the first day."

"Really?" Augusta asked.

The man nodded, and Chrisna couldn't help but grin at his proud expression.

"I heard you say you're from Little Rock," the black-haired woman said to Augusta.

"Darn tootin'," Augusta said in her high-pitched voice.

"Then we're neighbors." The black-haired women smiled. "We're from Jacksonville."

Augusta pushed past her husband to get to the woman. "Well, hi ya'll."

Chrisna looked at Jed, who sighed deeply.

The line moved again and, for a while, Chrisna listened to the loud conversation between Augusta and the black-haired woman. They talked about the Fourth of July celebrations they were going to miss, and how the black-haired woman and her husband would go to Little Rock each year for Pops on the River. Apparently they loved the orchestra that played patriotic music.

Chrisna shuffled forward and her stomach growled. She then realized that the only things she had eaten all day was the cookie and the croissant Tyce had bought for her and that was almost six hours ago. Her chest tightened a little but she shrugged off the thought of regret. She was seizing the moment now.

There didn't seem to be any refreshment stands around, only hordes and hordes of people blocking her view, so she waited.

Gradually, the queue moved forward. Every now and again, she would check her watch; 8.11pm...8.38pm...-

8.47pm…8.52pm… She'd finally reached the guardrails but there were still a lot of people in front of her. Her feet ached and she shifted from one foot to the other.

It was still light out but she suddenly felt tired. Her tongue stuck to the roof of her mouth and she felt like kicking herself for not bringing along a bottle of water.

At 9.15pm, she looked at the two dozen people still ahead of her in the queue.

Pulling her Paris guidebook from her purse, she read some facts on the Eiffel Tower. '*The Eiffel Tower is a lattice iron tower, engineered by Gustave Eiffel, whose company designed and built the tower. Erected in 1889…one of the most recognizable structures in the world, standing at 324 meters (1,063 ft) tall…*'

At 9.45pm, she finally reached the steps to the ticket office and she felt excited again.

There were only a few people still ahead of her in the queue, but the man in front suddenly started yelling at the ticket vendor in a foreign language before stomping down the stairs. As he passed by Chrisna, she heard him say, "Stupide persone Francesi!"

The sun started to set and a few minutes later, an amber glow filled the sky. She looked up through the steel beams again and thought about how amazing the Paris sunset must look from 324 meters up in the air.

Finally, it was her turn and she hurried to the ticket vendor. "One ticket to the top, please," she said.

The petite young woman shook her head. "No. Only ticketz to ze second floor," she said in a French accent.

"What? Why?"

"Zis is for ze stairs but ticketz to ze top end at nine-tirty." The woman pointed to the ticket office across the way where the longer queue had been earlier. "Elevators are clozed."

Chrisna saw an information board behind the woman, showing that all ticket sales close at 10pm. She looked at her watch, 9.55pm. Glancing back over her shoulder, she noticed that there weren't anyone else in line behind the broad-shouldered man and his wife. She sighed. At least she'll be able to go up. "One, please."

Disappointed, she paid the vendor and headed to the staircase.

Every now and again, she would glance down at the people on the ground getting smaller and smaller as she ascended the steps.

About halfway to the first floor, she stopped and took a breath. She felt more tired than she thought she would.

Augusta came up the stairs with Jed a few steps behind her, still carrying the backpack and holding onto the white bags.

"He hadn't counted on it being so many steps." Augusta panted as she stopped next to Chrisna. "How you doing? Taking a breather?"

Chrisna nodded and looked at Jed struggling up the stairs. When he passed by them, he missed a step and almost fell.

Augusta glanced at him. "You all right there, honey?"

Jed merely grunted and hiked forward.

"He's so clumsy he could trip over a cordless phone," Augusta said and turned to Chrisna. "Lovely view, ain't it?"

Chrisna looked at the city lights that had come on. The amber glow was disappearing fast and the view was breathtaking.

"Well, no time to dilly-dally," Augusta said and headed up the stairs again.

Taking a deep breath, Chrisna counted the steps she took.

One hundred and sixty-four steps later, she had reached the first floor and had to stop to rest for a minute before making her way to the buffet.

Standing in line for another fifteen minutes didn't bother her as much as the small fortune she had to pay for two bottles of water and authentic French Fries.

She placed one of the bottles in her purse, as she gulped down the cold liquid from the other, instantly feeling rejuvenated, and then ate the whole carton of thick salty fries.

Circling the first floor, she pushed through the tourists and disregarded the souvenir shop as she stared at the magnificent view of blue, white, and yellow lights that carpeted the capital. She stopped and touched the mesh-wire fence. If she wanted to, she could throw her ring off right there and then, but it didn't feel right. It wasn't how she expected it would be. She didn't feel half as excited about it as she had a few hours earlier.

She pulled the guidebook from her purse and flipped to the pages on the Eiffel Tower. She was only 58 meters off the ground and although it was high, the hotel in Cape Town in which she stayed with her husband during their honeymoon, was much taller than that.

She glanced at the dainty gold band with the beautiful setting, and then read further down on the page and saw that the second floor was approximately double the height of the first. Maybe that would make a difference.

Putting the book away, she headed to the staircase again, but Augusta intercepted her.

"Fancy seein' you again," Augusta said.

"Are you going up to the second floor?" Chrisna asked, noticing Jed looking worried when he glanced up.

"Nah, Jed's tuckered out. Are *you* going up?"

Quickly glancing at her ring again, Chrisna took a breath. "I guess I am."

"Well, enjoy the rest of your trip. Go hog wild." Augusta smiled and headed down the stairs.

"Bye," Chrisna said. "Bye, Jed." She gave him an encouraging smile when he plodded past her, and this time, he actually smiled back.

"Come on, honey!" Augusta yelled in her thick Southern accent, and Jed's smile disappeared.

Chrisna looked up at the staircase and only then noticed the black numbers on the sides, indicating the number of steps.

No. 450: She stopped to rest for a few minutes. It was getting colder and rather windy.

No. 575: She drank half the water from the bottle in her purse.

No. 624: She stopped again when lights started flickering on the outside of the beams, and she could hear people clapping and cheering.

Racing up the last forty-five steps to the second floor, she saw the area by the mesh-wire fence packed with tourists gazing up and taking photos of the outside of the top structure.

She could not see through the crowds, so she hurried past the masses, looking for a gap.

When she finally found a spot, the lights flickered once more and then went out.

The crowd dispersed in a drone of excitement and Chrisna bent down, placed her hands on her knees, and tried to catch her breath. She could hear her heart beating in her ears and her legs trembled. Feeling slightly nauseated and dizzy when she stood up again, she took a few sips of her water and walked closer to the fence.

From higher up, the lights merely looked farther away and there were more of them, a lot more, but she couldn't force herself to get excited about what she was about to do. If anything, she felt alone.

As she returned the water bottle to her purse, she pushed the strap up onto her shoulder, removed her wedding ring, and breathed out. The more she thought about what getting rid of the ring signified, the harder she found it to swallow as her throat tightened. She knew she didn't have a choice if she was going to close the chapter on that part of her life. A part of her life that had been over for a long time, she just needed to let it go, to let *him* go.

Chrisna removed her glasses, and wiped her eyes with the back of her hand.

Could she actually do it?

Breathing in deeply, she pushed her glasses back onto her nose and gripped the teardrop sapphire necklace in her hand. If she was going to do it, there was only one way, and it wasn't flinging it off the second floor.

She pushed the ring back onto her finger, clenched her jaw and returned to the staircase.

Four

"One elevator ticket to the top, please," Chrisna said and sighed with relief when she handed the vendor the money and received her ticket.

It was 10.09am on a warm sunny morning when she reached the front of the queue to the elevators, glad that she'd woken up early to be near the front of the ticket line at the Eiffel Tower.

This time she had set her intentions, and she didn't want to deviate from it for anything. She'd go straight to the top, fling her ring over the side, and then grab something to eat on her way to meet Zenelda at the Arc de Triomphe at one. She'd already amended her itinerary to fit in all the sites she'd missed into Saturday. As a result, the rest of her Friday was free to spend some time at the festival.

More than prepared, with two bottles of water in her purse, a fully charged cell phone, and the sapphire necklace around her neck, she anxiously waited for the elevator doors to open as she rubbed the blue stone with her thumb.

The shade of blue, coincidentally, matched the outfit

she had planned to wear for that day perfectly; black jeans, a baby-blue sleeveless collar-blouse, and black ballet pumps.

The doors of the yellow elevator opened and she hurried in first, standing against the far glass wall. Many people pushed in after her before the doors closed and they ascended the tracks. Chrisna could feel the butterflies fluttering around in her stomach.

The people around her spoke in various languages, but the overall tone were the same as the ground pulled farther and farther away – excitement.

The horizontal trusses passed by the glass wall in three-second intervals and the buildings below transformed into a cream-colored ocean.

Chrisna pulled her phone from her purse and took a few photos. The pictures didn't do justice to the mesmerizing landscape, so she switched it to video camera mode.

The elevator slowed down, stopped on the second level, and a loud beeping sound echoed through the small space. The people stood herded together, waiting for the doors to open.

"Are we stuck?" a man holding an infant asked after a few seconds.

The longer the beeping continued, the more restless the people became, and the baby started wailing when a man slammed his palm against the doors. Chrisna jumped and then heard the man yell, "Vamos sair!"

"I can't be stuck in here," someone said.

"And we can?" someone else asked in a tense tone.

"Help!" a woman holding onto a stroller yelled, and then another person yelled, and another.

Chrisna felt her heart pounding against her chest and she tried to swallow away the tightening feeling in her throat.

A bushy-haired man with a red beanie, a thick beard, and silver-rimmed glasses, that looked to be in his sixties, started humming next to her before he softly started to sing to himself. "*Well this is just great, I gotta say. Stuck in an elevator, it just ain't my day.*" He sang a little louder. "*Well this is just great, I gotta say. Stuck in an elevator, it just ain't my day.*"

Chrisna thought she recognized the melody but not the words, and she knew the man must have been making them up.

Then he belted out, "*Help, help, help, help, help.*"

He started off on a high note and then descended to a very low tone as he repeated, "*Help, help, help, help, help.*"

Everyone turned quiet, and even the baby stopped crying, as they listened to the bushy-haired man stomping his foot and clapping his hands to the rhythm of his singing.

Lifting her phone, Chrisna saw that she was still recording and she pointed the lens at the man.

"*Well this is just great, I gotta say. Stuck in an elevator, it just ain't my day.*" The man sang the same words to the simple melody again.

Chrisna couldn't help but join in when he sang, "*Help, help, help, help, help.*"

Soon, almost everyone was clapping along as the man continued to sing the first verse and, at what she now considered to be the chorus, they all belted out in unison, "*Help, help, help, help, help.*"

The group broke out in thunderous applause when the man stomped his foot one last time and ended the song.

Chrisna stopped the recording and returned her phone to her purse as the bushy-haired man removed his beanie and took a bow.

After the excitement had died down, there was almost a full minute of silence, and Chrisna could feel the tension building again. She gave the bushy-haired man a pleading look, but he smiled a skew smile and then held out the beanie, shaking it at her.

She reached into her purse and pulled out her wallet, unzipped the change pocket, took out a fifty cent coin and dropped it into the hat.

The man glared at the coin and then shook his head.

A quick glance told her that the people were getting more and more anxious, so she took out two Euro-coins and placed it in the hat. The man grinned, placed the hat by his feet and started clapping again. Kicking off with, "*This isn't ideal, I feel what you feel, but we can't do anything about it...*" He continued to sing the relevant words to a catchy tune, and soon everyone was clapping again and trying to sing along.

Chrisna watched him perform and captivate the people, the tension fading away, if only for a moment. He was good, very good, and as she sang along, she wondered if this counted as Zenelda's 'Sing in front of a crowd' task. She peaked at the list, *3. Sing in front of a crowd of at least fifty people.*

Fifty people? She counted but there were only about twenty other people in the elevator with her. Surely, it had to count. She smiled and she mentally checked it off the list.

Halfway through the second chorus of "*Let me off this damn elevator, let me out. Let me off, I mean it, let me out…*" the elevator doors opened and everyone cheered, including a crowd that was standing outside the doors.

Chrisna turned to the man, who picked up his beanie with only her two Euros and fifty cent in it, and she handed him a Five Euro bill and shook his hand. "Thank you," she said and stepped off the elevator onto the second floor.

The crowd had dispersed and everyone headed in their own directions.

Chrisna looked at a mass of people waiting to get onto another elevator, and glancing at her watch that indicated 10.49am, she walked to the end of the line on the side of the tower facing the Seine, and waited. If it didn't take too long to get to the top, she was still on schedule to meet Zenelda at one. She looked at the sapphire pendant. Why would someone give a complete stranger a family heirloom and trust them to return it?

After about ten minutes, she was almost at the front, when she heard two women behind her discussing the view from the top.

She turned around. "Isn't this the line to go up?"

"No, we're going down. You have to take the other elevator."

Feeling a little embarrassed, Chrisna quickly left the queue, and only then noticed a sign indicating in which direction she should go. She followed the ropes to the outside perimeter, and found another spiraling line of even more people, condensed into a small area near the center of the tower.

11.18am…11.39am…12.04pm…

She wasn't going to make it. Even if she could get onto the next elevator, which didn't seem likely, she'd still have to queue to get down again.

Chrisna pulled the gold chain away from her chest, looked at the pendant, then at her wedding ring, and back at the pendant again. She had to return the necklace to Zenelda. The guilt would haunt her if she didn't.

She glanced at her ring again, feeling the same melancholy she had felt the night before, when she thought back to her honeymoon, pushing against her chest. Something prevented her from getting rid of her ring. It had been just too difficult.

When she stepped out of line and walked back to the queue she'd been in earlier, it had almost doubled in length. She took a breath and fell in behind the last person.

Every minute that passed felt longer than the one before, and she checked her watch every few minutes calculating whether she would make it to Zenelda on time.

There was no time left for her to walk to the Arc de Triomphe as she'd planned and she hadn't worked out the bus route. Maybe she could take the train.

Pulling the Metro map from her purse, she stared in confusion at the jumble of colored lines. She didn't plan for this. According to her itinerary, she would only use the Metro on Day 3, and although it was her third day in Paris, she'd not completed Day 2's activities yet.

"Do you need some help?" a man standing behind her asked when she turned the map around for the second time.

He looked young with his spiky blond hair and bright yellow t-shirt with '*BARCA*' printed in bold black letters on the front.

"Please." She handed him the map and pushed her glasses up on her nose. "I need to go to the Arc de Triomphe."

He smiled. "You should just walk. It'll only take you half an hour."

"That was the plan but I'm in a hurry now."

He examined the map. "The best way is to go to Trocadéro station. That's about fifteen minutes from here." He pointed to a small white dot where a green line and dark yellow line crossed. "Get off at Kléber. It's the second stop. The Arc de Triomphe is five minutes' walk from there."

"Thank you," Chrisna said, took the map from him, and stared at the colored lines, searching for the white dot. "Maybe I should just take a taxi."

"The *Mettre en Valeur* starts today. If you're lucky enough to get a taxi, you'll be stuck in traffic," he said. "The Metro's going to be chaos as well. My advice is, run for it." He smiled.

The elevator ride to the bottom couldn't go fast enough and Chrisna looked at the itinerary on her phone. Maybe she should just go back to her planned schedule. Deviating from her timetable has caused nothing but trouble.

When the doors opened on the ground floor, she checked the time again, 12.43pm.

"Good luck," the spiky-haired guy said as she stepped out of the elevator.

With her phone still in hand, now opened on the GPS App. she'd used to work out her route the previous night, she held on tightly to her purse, and sprinted to the intersection of Quai Branly and Pont d'Iéna.

Running on the outside of the Zebra crossing, she tried to pass the hordes of people on their way to the Eiffel Tower.

A man on a bicycle almost ran her over when she raced over the bridge to the other side of the Seine. It took long enough to cross for her to see the boats lined up on both sides of the river, and Tyce popped into her head again.

She almost stepped in front of a yellow tour bus that turned the corner at Port Debilly in her rush to cross the street. She glanced at the words, '*2 day Pass 2 jours*', when it passed by her.

Not sure in which direction to head at the next big intersection, she took some time to catch her breath while finding her way.

After passing a couple of souvenir stands, she entered a smaller street with trees towering on either side. She looked at the brick road, then up at the clear blue sky, and then down at her ballet pumps as she jogged on the concrete sidewalk, wishing that she'd rather chosen to wear her trainers again.

Buildings gradually replaced the trees as she crossed another intersection and slowed down. Every now and again, she had to walk around guardrails that blocked the sidewalk, so she crossed the street to where there was more space.

Stopping to sit down on a bus bench, she placed her hands on her knees and tried to catch her breath again. Taking a bottle of water from her purse, she finished most of it and then looked at her phone. She'd almost covered half of the distance to the Arc de Triomphe.

Checking the time, 12.53pm, she knew she was going to be late.

She leaped up from the bench and set off again, walking briskly as she rounded a massive intersection with a statue of a man on a horse, holding a sword.

She continued down Avenue d'Iéna, and the traffic

became more congested and cars were parked, bumper to bumper, on either side of the street.

Her feet felt heavy as she pushed herself to continue, but at a much slower pace.

Amazed at how many scooters there were on the road and parked alongside the street, she sprinted through a gap in the traffic at the next intersection, and a motorist driving a white Volkswagen, honked his horn. "Skees!" she yelled and continued down the tree-lined street.

Half way down the next block, she sighed with relief when she saw the monumental archway peeking through the trees. 1.05pm, and she hated being late.

Stopping on the outside of a massive circle with the Arc de Triomphe in the center, she saw cars, busses, and scooters racing in a loop, and she couldn't understand how they didn't crash into each other as they entered and exited at an alarming speed.

She passed behind the vehicles parked on the outside, and rounded Place Charles de Gaulle and crossed a connecting street.

Her destination was right there but she still couldn't see a pedestrian crossing.

"How do I get to the Arc de Triomphe?" she asked an elderly couple, sitting on a bus bench.

The man frowned and lifted his brown fedora. "C'est par là," he mumbled and pointed to the enormous archway.

1.17pm. She was back at the same spot where she'd started.

She took a deep breath, gripped her purse under her arm, looked for an opening, and ran toward the inner circle. The motorists honked as she sidestepped cars, busses, and a scooter that only just missed her. One driver yelled, "Idiot!" as she stepped onto the curb, her heart racing.

Breathing heavily, she untied her ponytail, pushed her fingers through the damp strands above her ears, and then fastened her hair back tightly.

She took a small make-up mirror from her purse, wiped her face with a tissue, and applied lip-gloss before returning the mirror to her bag. She took out a small roll-on deodorant bottle, and bending over, she pushed her hand in underneath the hem of her blouse and rolled the gel over the skin of her underarms.

She turned away from the people standing around the stone monument, and heard a loud honking. When she looked up, a man in a black car whistled as he drove by.

She looked down at her blouse, only then realizing that the top button had come undone and in her bent position, her blue bra was showing. She blushed quickly pushing her hand against her chest, stood upright, turned around, and fastened the button before returning the deodorant to her purse.

Stepping over a thick, low-hanging chain attached to black-metal ball posts that circled the area around the monument, she headed in the direction of the gigantic, blue, white, and red flag, hanging from the middle of the arch. She pushed through a large number of tourists, gazing up at the structure. How was she ever going to find Zenelda in this crowd?

Walking to a roped-off area in the center of the arch, she saw a billowing flame burning on top of a round golden disc, encircled by various shaped wreaths in the colors of the French flag.

"It's an eternal flame," someone whispered in her ear, and she swung around to see Zenelda, dressed in dark blue jeans, a multicolored belt, and a tight white t-shirt. The wooden beads from an assortment of necklaces obscured a few of the letters on her shirt that read, '*I listen to bands that don't even exist yet*'.

"Eternal flame," Zenelda repeated and took off her black and white striped-rim sunglasses, revealing purple-gray eye shadow, which made her cobalt eyes look smoky. "Makes me think of this band I used to know." She adjusted the gray newsboy cap on top of her fiery red hair and sighed. "We had a bitchin' summer."

"I'm sorry I'm late," Chrisna said.

Zenelda looked closely at her bare wrist, tapped the skin with her index finger, and then held her wrist up to her ear. "I hadn't noticed."

Chrisna unclasped the necklace and held it out to Zenelda. "I think its luck's run out."

Fiddling with the leather tassels hanging from a small leather pouch below her left hip, Zenelda grinned and ran her fingers up the thin leather strap that hung over her shoulder. "You keep it. It goes great with your outfit."

Chrisna looked at the sapphire. "No, I couldn't, it's too valuable."

Zenelda snickered. "I bought that at a costume jewelry stand a couple of weeks ago. Only cost me something like three pounds. I think the stone's made of glass." She looked down, lifted her right foot, and pointed to the gold-studded red leather boot. "The same flea market I bought these boots at. Nice, huh?"

"What?" Chrisna gaped at her. "Then why did you tell me it was a family heirloom?"

Zenelda placed her sunglasses back on her face. "I wanted you to come to the festival with me, and obviously it worked."

"But I ran here," she said, feeling suddenly angry.

"Not to worry, we can walk slowly if you want. I actually prefer it, allows me to take in—"

"I'm not going with you now." Chrisna raised her voice and held the necklace out to her again. "Here, take it."

"No I can't. It's bad luck to take back a gift after it's been given."

"Take it."

"No."

"Fine then." Chrisna placed the necklace on the ground between them. "And you can have this back as well." Reaching into her purse, she pulled the silver coin from the small compartment, and placed it on the ground next to the necklace. "Good-bye," she said and stomped off.

"I didn't give you the coin!" Zenelda called after her.

Chrisna stopped and turned around, taking a breath before walking back to where Zenelda stood. When she reached her, Zenelda held the necklace up in one hand and the coin in the other.

"Then give it back." Chrisna held out her hand and Zenelda placed the coin on her palm.

"You don't know what that is, do you?" Zenelda asked.

"Do *you*?" Chrisna looked at the engravings of the eight-point star and three flowers.

"No, but I might know someone who does."

Chrisna looked up at her. "Who?"

"I'll take you to him. Come on." Zenelda smiled mysteriously and then turned around, walking past the memorial.

Chrisna glanced at the coin again. "Can't you just call him?"

"Just like me, he doesn't believe in cell phones," Zenelda yelled, not stopping.

Chrisna shoved the coin back into her purse, adjusted the strap over her shoulder and walked quickly to try to catch up to Zenelda.

Keeping Zenelda in her sight, she pushed through the crowd, looking up every chance she got to gaze at the stone carvings on the arched roof. When she looked down again, Zenelda had disappeared in the crowds yet again. She arched her feet, stretching to try to see over the hordes of people, and continued in the direction in which Zenelda had headed.

Then she stopped and looked down at a flight of stairs, leading underground. Zenelda waited halfway down the steps. "Come on," she said and walked down.

Rushing down the steps, Chrisna caught up with Zenelda in the ominously lit passageway. "Where are we going?" Her voice echoed.

"Champs-Élysées."

"Okay," she said, softer this time.

After going up another flight of stairs and exiting onto a busy street corner, Chrisna turned around and saw the Arc de Triomphe across street. She remembered passing that corner when she'd searched for a way to get to the monument. How did she miss the passageway?

"You get distracted quite easily, don't you?" Zenelda asked. "Ooh, ice cream." She hurried to a pink stand with '*Glaces*' written on the sign.

Chrisna stared after her.

"You want one?" Zenelda yelled.

Quickly walking to where Zenelda stood in a short queue, Chrisna waited until she'd reached her to answer, "No, thank you, I don't like ice cream."

"Boom!" Zenelda gaped at her. "Who doesn't like ice cream?"

Chrisna frowned. "Lots of people."

"Name one."

"What can I get for you?" the vendor asked, pushing the sleeves of his white coat up his forearms.

Zenelda pushed herself up onto the balls of her feet, placed her elbows on the counter, and peaked in. "A pink swirly with lots of red syrup." She looked excited.

The man pushed a cone in underneath a metal nozzle and pulled the lever, twirling the cone as the ice cream streamed into it. Squirting the red syrup on top, he handed the cone to Zenelda, who paid him.

"It looks good," Chrisna said when Zenelda took a mouthful off the top.

"Then get one."

Chrisna shook her head and pulled a face. "No, thank you."

"I don't get you."

"I don't like ice cream but I like the way it looks," Chrisna said, pulling the bottle of water out of her purse and taking a sip.

Zenelda grinned.

Halfway down the block, they crossed to the other side of Champs-Élysées and continued down the broader sidewalk. Chrisna looked up at the large metal and glass building on her right.

"I love buildings like that," Zenelda said. "It screams, *Look at me! I'm different!*" She threw her arms up in the air, twirled, and her ice cream flew off the cone.

"What are you doing?" Chrisna asked shocked.

Zenelda looked at the ice cream on the ground and shrugged. "The cone is the best part anyway," she said and took a large bite.

"You, um, have something…" Chrisna pointed to a

spot on her own blouse, near her right hip.

Pulling her t-shirt away from her body, Zenelda looked at the pink stain on the white fabric, and then bent over and started licking the stain.

"You can't do that," Chrisna shrieked, placed the empty water bottle back in her purse, and pulled out a packet of wet wipes. "Here, let me help you." Bending down, she took the material in one hand and wiped the moist cloth over the stain in circular motions.

"Thanks mom," Zenelda mumbled.

Feeling a little embarrassed, Chrisna stood up. "I worked at a primary school for a while."

"That must've been fun."

"Do you like kids?" Chrisna asked and walked over to a trashcan, pulling the empty water bottle from her purse and dropping the bottle and the wet wipe in the bin.

"I love toys."

Chrisna frowned.

"You really should recycle," Zenelda said and set off down the busy sidewalk again.

The farther they walked, the busier the sidewalk became. Crowds streamed in and out of the shops and Chrisna struggled to sidestep all the people.

Zenelda suddenly stopped and waited for her to catch up. "What are you doing?"

"I'm walking."

"That's not walking. You can't zigzag like that. We'll be stuck here the whole day."

Chrisna turned sideways to allow another person to pass her. "There are too many people. I can't walk through them."

Zenelda grinned. "If you don't give way, *they* will." She pulled her shoulders back and charged through the crowd.

Chrisna sighed, pulled her shoulders back and briskly walked to catch up to Zenelda. A few times, she briefly closed her eyes when it looked as if someone was going to bump into her, but they never did.

"See," Zenelda said when Chrisna caught up to her. "They can sense you're not going to move."

Just then, someone bumped Chrisna's shoulder and the force flung her to the ground.

"That guy's senses must be off," Zenelda said as she held out her hand to Chrisna, helping her to stand. "You okay?"

Dusting off her jeans, Chrisna growled. "How far until we reach your friend?"

"Not too far."

They crossed a narrow side street with a long row of scooters parked on the one side, and identical bicycles with metal baskets on the front, on the other side.

"We should've had bicycles," Chrisna said and cursed her impractical choice of footwear again.

"You can rent those, you know," Zenelda said.

"Really? Then why don't we?"

Zenelda kept walking. "I don't do bicycles."

"What?" Chrisna hurried to catch up to her again.

"Why not?"

"Just because." Zenelda didn't look at her.

"Wait a second. You don't know how to ride a bicycle?"

"I didn't say that." Zenelda almost sounded angry. "I just don't like them. Give me a Fat Bob and I'll show you what riding is."

"A Fat Bob?"

"Harley Davidson, preferably a black '85 model. I learned to ride one in the summer of '95, just before I joined Boss's tour."

Chrisna frowned. "Boss?"

"Yes, as in Rick. The famous guitar..." She waited for a reaction but received merely a blank expression from Chrisna. "Wow." She shook her head. "Have you ever been on one?"

"A Fat boss?"

Zenelda snorted as she laughed. "It's a Fat Bob, and no, I meant any kind of bike."

Chrisna shook her head.

"You're missing out, sweetie."

Continuing down the sidewalk, Chrisna glanced at the variety of stores.

"Impressive, right?" Zenelda asked. "It's probably one of the most famous streets in the world, and the name is French for Elysian Fields, the place of the blessed dead in Greek mythology. If you were heroic, the gods would choose you to have a happy afterlife, pampering you with whatever you enjoyed while you were still alive." She grinned. "I'll probably be touring with Blades of Blue in the afterlife, if it pleases the gods."

"Have you toured with Blades of Blue?" Chrisna asked wide-eyed. "I love them."

"Very briefly. I met them when Extreme opened for them. But I left to hang out with Primus for a while after that."

Chrisna wasn't sure how to react to that. Blades of Blue was probably her favorite band of all time. She had shed many tears while listening to '*Scattered Tears*' repeatedly, after her divorce.

"Are you okay?" Zenelda asked.

Chrisna hadn't even realized that she'd stopped walking. She cleared her throat. "Ja, I'm fine."

"Why don't I believe you?"

"I was just thinking. That's all."

"A dangerous pastime." Zenelda smiled. "You have to distract yourself when your thoughts threaten to take over. Come on."

"Where?"

"You'll see." Zenelda grabbed her hand and pulled her down the sidewalk.

"Wait, where are we going?" Chrisna asked, trying to keep up with the long strides.

Zenelda didn't answer as she pulled her past a couple of four-storey buildings, past three restaurants, over two side streets, and past a coffee shop, before they stopped.

Chrisna pulled her hand out of Zenelda's grip. "What are you doing?"

"Distracting you, come on." Zenelda entered a tall, gray building with a large red, white, and blue sign above the door, reading, '*Seuls Jouets*'.

Chrisna followed her inside, staring at the numerous shelves of children's toys. There were shelves just for stuffed animals, others just for toy cars, dolls, board games, and building blocks. Several bins filled with a colorful selection of balls, stood near the ends of the aisles, and in the one corner there were replicas of characters from children's movies.

"Pick something," Zenelda said and removed her sunglasses, pushing the arm through her multicolored belt near her pocket.

"What?"

"Pick your favorite toy you had as a child and I'll buy it for you."

Thinking for a moment, Chrisna said, "We won't find that here."

"What was it?" Zenelda asked, looking intrigued.

"Sandra's parents' house used to have this long hallway where we would sit at each end of it, and talk to each other through two cans linked with a long piece of string." Chrisna smiled. "We even did that all through high school. It was our way of telling each other secrets. We weren't allowed to repeat anything that was said through those cans."

"I like that." Zenelda grinned. "But you're probably right. I don't think they'll have that here." She picked up an orange-colored ball from a nearby bin and played with it. "Then get something you've always wanted."

"No, it's okay. I don't want you to—"

"I insist." Zenelda said and headed down one of the aisles.

Chrisna watched her as she picked up and played with several of the toys before returning them to the shelf. She followed her for a while, but when she saw a spiraling metal staircase with red, white, and blue helium balloons attached to it, she ascended the steps to the second floor.

Rows and rows of children's fantasy costumes hung from metal railings. There were princess outfits, pirate outfits, and even super hero outfits.

Descending the stairs again a few minutes later, she stopped halfway down to look at the store from higher up. It was bigger than she'd thought. Toy planes and helicopters hung from the ceiling, and large stuffed animals were stacked on top of the shelves. She saw Zenelda walking down one of the aisles, heading in her direction. Hurrying down the steps, she headed in the opposite direction and browsed one of the shelves, trying to find something small and inexpensive.

"You found something?"

When Zenelda reached her, she picked up the first thing she saw and turned to her. "Ja."

"What is it?" Zenelda asked overly excited.

Chrisna held out her hand.

"Really? You never had one of those as a child?"

Glancing down at the kaleidoscope tube, Chrisna

grinned. "No," she said and she wasn't lying. "If you don't count the one I'd made out of a toilet paper tube in kindergarten."

"Okay then," Zenelda said. "Come on, we still have a couple of blocks to go."

"Do you think they have a bathroom here?"

"No," Zenelda grinned. "But they have a toilet. Somewhat of a necessity if you consider their target market. It's just down there." She pointed to a small corridor near the tellers. "I'll hold your purse for you."

Chrisna hesitated. "No, it's okay. But if you wouldn't mind holding this," she said, handing Zenelda the kaleidoscope tube and hurrying to the toilet.

When she was done, she saw a small boy of about five, bouncing up and down outside the door. "Skees," she said and caught up to Zenelda, waiting in the queue.

When they reached the teller, Chrisna placed her purse on the counter and took out her wallet.

Zenelda frowned. "What are you doing? I said I'd pay."

"I can't let you do that," Chrisna said, feeling uncomfortable.

"You're not *letting* me. Call it a peace offering for lying to you about the necklace."

Sighing, Chrisna returned her wallet to her bag. "Okay. Thank you."

The teller took the kaleidoscope tube from Chrisna and frowned as she turned it around in her hand. "I'm sorry, there's no bar code on this." She reached over and pressed a button. "Contrôle des prix, contre deux," she said into the microphone and then turned back to them. "It will only take a minute. Will this be all?"

"Yes," Zenelda said and smiled.

They waited for a while and Chrisna glanced back at the long line forming behind them. "I can go get another one. I know where they are." She didn't give the teller a chance to respond before speeding to the shelf where she'd found the tube earlier, and seconds later, she was back at the counter. "Here you go." She handed the teller the toy.

The teller scanned the item and placed it into a white bag.

"Thank you," Chrisna said, taking the bag from the teller and picking up her purse off the counter, flinging the strap over her shoulder.

"Here," Zenelda said, handing Chrisna the receipt. "They check it at the door."

Chrisna opened the bag and held out the receipt when they'd reached the door. The security guard checked the contents of the bag and then nodded, but when they stepped through the door, an alarm sounded.

Chrisna stopped and turned around to see the security guard standing behind them.

"May I check your purse?" the man asked.

"Sure," Chrisna said, feeling her cheeks heat up as some of the people in the store stared at her.

"I wouldn't do that if I were you," Zenelda said.

"No, it's okay," Chrisna said. But then the security

guard pulled a small carton box, containing two tiny walkie-talkies with butterflies printed on them, from her purse. "I didn't take that," she said shocked and looked at Zenelda.

"Please come with me," the security guard said.

"I told you," Zenelda said and grabbed the box from the man, pushed it into Chrisna's hands and shouted, "Run, Kristal!"

The guard reached for her arm, but Chrisna stepped back and sprinted after Zenelda, who was already half-way down the block.

Five

Struggling to keep up with Zenelda, Chrisna ran to the large intersection at the end of the block, and then Zenelda turned right and left again at the first narrow street. Zenelda glanced back a few times while holding her hat in place on her head, but Chrisna kept looking straight in front of her, her heart racing. They ran in the middle of the narrow street, passing another long line of motorcycles and bicycles parked on the sides of the road, and then Zenelda stopped, grabbed Chrisna's arm as she passed by and held on tightly, almost flinging her to the ground.

"Have you lost your mind?" Chrisna panted and pushed her glasses up on the bridge of her nose.

Zenelda pulled her onto the curb and knocked on a bright green door.

"Let go of me." Chrisna pulled out of her grip and glanced up at the thin brown structure squeezed in between the two white four-storey buildings.

"Shhh, we have to be quiet now," Zenelda whispered and the door opened.

A large angry-looking black man towered over them

in a sleeveless white shirt. "What do you want?" he asked in a deep voice.

"All your money," Zenelda said.

"What?" Chrisna's heart skipped a beat.

The man grinned. "Well, come on in then."

Zenelda reached up and hugged the man tightly. "I've missed you, Aman."

"Where've you been?" he asked as he escorted Zenelda through the door.

Chrisna stood frozen as she stared after them.

They stopped and looked back at her. "What's up with your friend?" Aman asked.

"She's a strange one, alright," Zenelda said and waved Chrisna in.

"*I'm* the strange one?" Chrisna mumbled under her breath as she followed them.

A few small round tables stood around a circular wooden bar counter in the middle of the dimly lit room. A large Jamaican flag hung from the ceiling and graffiti covered the yellow walls. One phrase caught her eye, '*If you're not here, then where are you?*'

Chrisna noticed that everyone in the room was black and some of the men sported long dreadlocks. Their stares followed her as she followed Zenelda and Aman to the bar counter.

"Have a seat," Aman said. "First round's on me."

Chrisna shifted onto the high barstool next to Zenelda and whispered, "I don't think we should be in here."

"Why not?" Zenelda asked loudly.

"We don't, um, fit," Chrisna whispered again.

Zenelda smiled. "Oh, don't worry, sweetie. Not everyone in here is Jamaican."

Chrisna shifted in her seat when Aman stared at her. "What can I get for you?" he asked.

"Just water, please." Chrisna forced a grin, and she heard a few of the men at the bar snicker.

"I only serve water if it's mixed with alcohol," Aman said in his deep voice.

"We'll both have a beer, thanks," Zenelda said, and he turned around to get the drinks.

"I don't drink beer," Chrisna whispered.

Zenelda frowned. "Well, I wouldn't suggest asking for wine in this place, it's worse than trying to ask for water."

Chrisna looked down at her hands, only then realizing that she was still tightly holding onto the white bag with one hand, and the box with the walkie-talkies was clutched in the other.

Zenelda took the box from her and placed it on the counter. "Don't worry. No cop ever comes in here."

"Why did you steal that?" Chrisna asked softly, placing the white bag with the kaleidoscope tube in her purse, which she gripped tightly on her lap while glancing around the room.

Zenelda leaned in and whispered, "I didn't steal it, *you* did."

"What? No, you made me. You put it in my purse."

"Can you prove it?" Zenelda asked. "Besides, no one can make you do anything without your consent."

"We have to take it back."

"Why?"

Chrisna frowned. "Because it's a crime. You, um, *we* broke the law."

"And you've never broken the law before?"

"Of course not."

Aman placed two open bottles of beer, with red and white labels, on the counter in front of them.

"Can I have a glass?" Chrisna asked him, and he glared at her. "Never mind," she said and pulled a tissue from her purse, thoroughly wiping the top rim before taking a sip, and then pulling a face.

"She *is* strange," Aman said to Zenelda before turning to help another customer.

Zenelda smiled. "So you've never broken the law? Not ever?"

"No."

"Not even taking a piece of bubblegum without paying for it?" Zenelda took a big gulp of her beer.

"No."

"Not even a speeding ticket?"

"I said no." Chrisna took a small sip of her beer and cringed.

"So, how did it feel?"

"Like my heart was going to break through my chest. I wouldn't have been able to stop running if you hadn't grabbed me."

"That's called adrenalin," Zenelda said, taking another sip. "Best feeling in the world when you combine it with unadulterated fear."

Chrisna recalled how she'd felt after she'd hugged the Venus de Milo, but even that feeling of utter exhilaration couldn't get close to what she'd just felt. Her entire body still felt numb and tingly. She smiled.

"There we go. You just have to give in to it." Zenelda returned her smile.

Chrisna forced herself to stop smiling. "We still have to take it back."

"I don't think so. I got it for us."

"What? Why?"

Zenelda opened the box and handed her one of the walkie-talkies. "I thought you might like it. You know, like when you and your friend used to—"

"You're *not* my friend." Chrisna regretted what she said as she said it.

Zenelda turned serious. "No, I guess I'm not." She placed her walkie-talkie back into the box. "Come on, we'll go back and return it." She stood up.

Chrisna felt awful. "I didn't mean to—"

"No, you're right. We *should* take it back." She held out her hand, waiting for Chrisna to hand her the other walkie-talkie.

Looking at it, Chrisna considered the strange gesture. It was thoughtful, even though she'd stolen it. "Maybe we can finish our drinks and then go back and pay for it."

"Really?" Zenelda asked surprised. "You want to keep them?"

"Sure. I guess it would be fun, and it might help if I lose you in the crowd again, since you don't believe in cell phones."

Zenelda smiled and jumped back on the chair. "Great, but we don't have to go back to pay for them."

Chrisna frowned. "Ja, we do."

"No, we don't." She took a big sip of her beer. "I already paid for them." She pulled a receipt out of the leather pouch hanging near her hip and handed it to Chrisna. "See."

Looking at the receipt, Chrisna saw that it confirmed the purchase of one set of walkie-talkies. She gaped at Zenelda. "What? How? Why?"

"Boom!"

Chrisna jumped in her seat.

"I bought them when you were wandering 'round the store." She looked impressed with herself. "The manager's a good friend of mine, so it had all been arranged by the time I met up with you again. The only challenge was to get it into your purse, since you didn't trust me to hang onto it for you while you were in the toilet. Luckily, you left your purse on the counter when you went to get another one of those kaleidoscope thingies."

Chrisna stared at her.

"You're welcome," Zenelda said and took another sip.

"So we didn't steal it?"

"Technically, no, but you thought we did, and that was the point."

"What point?" Chrisna asked, raising her voice. "Scaring me half to death? Making me think that I was being chased?"

"Yeah, you have to admit, it was fun."

Chrisna took a few sips of her beer and then sighed deeply. "Switch on your walkie-talkie." She flipped the tiny switch on the side of hers and held it up to her mouth.

"Why?"

"I want to tell you a secret."

Zenelda pulled the walkie-talkie out of the box again and turned it on, holding it to her ear.

Pressing the yellow butterfly-shaped button, Chrisna whispered, "Jou kop raas."

Zenelda frowned. "What does that mean?"

"Roughly translated, it means your head is making noises. Simply put, you're crazy."

Zenelda smiled. "That's no secret, sweetie."

They both laughed.

"You guys doing okay over here?" Aman asked as he leaned over the counter.

"We're good," Chrisna said and smiled at Zenelda.

"Aman, can you look at something for me?" Zenelda asked and turned to Chrisna. "Hand me that coin." She placed the walkie-talkie in her pouch and left the box on the counter.

Chrisna opened her purse, pushed her walkie-talkie

into one of the compartments and pulled out the coin, handing it to her.

"Have you seen this before?" Zenelda asked, handing the coin to Aman.

He examined it for a while. "No, where did you get it?" He gave it back to Zenelda, who handed it to Chrisna.

"I found it in my purse yesterday morning." Chrisna sighed and turned to Zenelda. "Is *he* the friend you were telling me about?"

"No, I just took a shot in the dark," Zenelda said, and Aman left the counter. Taking another sip of her beer, she asked, "You sure you didn't bring it with you from South Africa?"

"I'm sure. I only found it yesterday, after the night I couldn't remember."

"Okay, wait! Backup. Explain," Zenelda said, looking intrigued.

Chrisna took a big gulp of her beer. She was starting to get used to the taste. "After I left the airport the other day, I went to my hotel, unpacked, and then went for dinner at a nearby restaurant, and that's all I can remember. Apparently, I met a guy at a music-bar and went to a party with him. I ran into him yesterday but he didn't know anything about the coin either." She took another sip.

"Boom!"

Chrisna jumped in her seat again and almost choked on the beer. She swallowed and wiped her mouth with the back of her hand. "You really should warn me before you do that."

"So what happened? Did you sleep with him?"

"No," Chrisna said shocked, and then thought about it for a minute. "Well, that's what he told me." Suddenly she wasn't all that sure.

"Was he hot at least?"

Chrisna felt her cheeks heat up. "He wasn't bad looking."

"Are you going to see him again?"

"No." She felt the regret push up her throat again and swallowed it down with another sip of beer.

"Why not?"

"You know that curiosity killed the cat, right?"

Zenelda smirked. "Death doesn't bother me. I'll be hanging out with The Cram Jammers."

"Blades of Blue."

"What?"

"You said Blades of Blue earlier."

"Yeah, them too." Zenelda grinned and took the last sip of her beer. "You're still wearing your ring I see."

Looking down at her wedding ring, Chrisna twirled it around her finger. "Ja. I couldn't do it."

"So you *are* still in love with him. Your husband?"

"Ex-husband. And no." She looked at Zenelda. "I tried to get up to the top of the Eiffel Tower but I had to come and meet you. I ran out of time, that's all," she said, not wanting to try to explain why she couldn't do it the first time, when she had the chance.

"Sorry 'bout that, but why then didn't you want to see that guy again? I can tell you like him. I've got a sense about things like that."

"Sixth sense?" Chrisna smiled.

"No."

Chrisna took the last sip of her beer. "It *is* called a sixth sense, isn't it?" She was starting to feel a little light-headed.

"The sixth sense is pain. The seventh is temperature." She tapped the tips of her fingers on her left hand as she counted. "Eight is balance, and nine is proprioception."

"What?"

"Body-awareness. Actually, there are a whole lot more of them. Twenty-one, I believe."

Chrisna frowned. "How do you know that?"

Zenelda looked offended for a second. "I read."

Aman placed a tumbler glass with dark liquid in front of each of them, and pointed his thumb in the direction of the far corner. Zenelda looked where he was pointing. "Oti!" she shrieked and ran over to an elderly black man with gray hair and a short gray beard, sitting on a stool in the corner, holding a cane. Everyone else in the room was casually dressed, most in bright colors, but he wore a plain brown suit and tie.

Chrisna watched as Zenelda hugged him and then continued to talk with him for a while. Every now and again, he glanced her way and she wondered what Zenelda was saying about her.

Waiting for Zenelda to return, Chrisna shifted uncomfortably in her seat. She glanced at the dark liquid in the short glass in front of her but didn't dare drink it. She shouldn't even have drunk that beer, not on an empty stomach.

Aman placed a small plate in front of her, and she looked at the four squared pieces of chocolate cake on it. "Thank you," she said and looked around for a fork, but there was none and she was too scared to ask Aman. She lifted one of the pieces with her fingers and took a bite. It was a little a dry, so she took a small sip from the tumbler to wash down the cake that was stuck in throat. The drink had a strong sweet coffee taste and she liked it. Taking another sip, she finished the rest of the piece of cake.

Zenelda returned to the counter a few minutes later and looked at the plate, and then at Chrisna.

"Sorry I didn't wait for you," Chrisna said, "but I hadn't had lunch yet."

Zenelda's eyes widened and she glared at Aman. "You didn't."

He grinned.

"What's wrong?" Chrisna asked.

Zenelda sat down next to her and took a deep breath. "Okay. I need to ask you a question but I don't want you to get upset."

"Okay," Chrisna said. "What is it?"

"Have you ever smoked pot before?"

"No," Chrisna said casually. "I don't smoke."

"I thought that's what you'd say." Zenelda almost

looked disappointed.

"Then why did you ask me?" Chrisna asked, and then her eyes widened. "Did you want me to smoke pot with you?"

It looked like Zenelda was trying to hide a grin. "Aw, sweetie, no, but you kinda already ingested some."

"Some what? Pot? No I…" Chrisna looked at the plate with the two remaining chocolate cake pieces on it and then looked at Zenelda. "Are those—?"

"Hash brownies, yes."

Chrisna gaped at Aman, who stood arms folded, grinning as he watched them. "You drugged me?" she asked, incredulously.

He just guffawed, shaking his head as he turned to serve another customer.

"Not cool, Aman," Zenelda said and took Chrisna's hand. "Now, I don't want you to worry. It's going to be okay."

"What will it do to me?" Chrisna asked anxiously.

"I can't really say. It's different for everyone. You might be fine." Zenelda didn't look convinced.

"Fine? I just took drugs." Chrisna felt her chest tighten.

"Okay, calm down. It's not drugs. It's just a little weed and you're with me. You. Will. Be. Fine." She accentuated the words. "Just relax." Turning to Aman, she said, "Bring her some water."

Aman growled, but Zenelda gave him a stern look, and he poured some water into a tall glass, handing it to her. Holding the glass out to Chrisna, she said, "Drink all of it. It'll help."

"You sure?" Chrisna asked, taking the glass.

"Of course. Would I lie to you?"

Chrisna glared at her before drinking all the water in the glass. She felt calmer and didn't feel any affects from the weed yet. Maybe it didn't affect her. "Let's go find that friend of yours," she said, placing the empty glass on the counter.

"Maybe I should take you back to your hotel," Zenelda said. "We can try again tomorrow."

"No, I have a lot to do tomorrow. I still have to visit the three museums I didn't get to see yesterday and I'm going to the Notre Dame and the Sacre-Coeur after that." She jumped off her chair. "Besides, I feel fine." She turned to Aman. "You were just messing with me right?"

Aman grinned. "Right."

Chrisna turned to Zenelda. "See, come on." She pulled her purse strap over her shoulder, raised the glass with the dark liquid, held it up in the direction of the elderly man in the corner, mouthed 'thank you', and took a big gulp, before placing it back on the counter.

"Why did you do that?" Zenelda asked, gaping at her.

"I didn't want to be rude."

Zenelda shook her head and quickly repeated what Chrisna had done, emptying her glass. "You sure you're feeling okay?" she asked as they left the bar.

"Ja, I'm fine," she said, pulling a pair of large brown-rimmed prescription sunglasses out of her purse and swapping them for the glasses she was wearing, when they stepped into the sunlight.

"Okay, let's do this," Zenelda said and pulled her sunglasses from her belt, pushing them onto her nose.

They walked back to Champs-Élysées with the hordes of people rushing up and down the sidewalk, most of them heading in the same direction they were going. Chrisna glanced back a couple of times and saw the Arc de Triomphe getting smaller behind them.

"It's hot today, isn't it?" Chrisna said.

"Yes." Zenelda glanced up at the clear blue sky. "A beautiful day. Think it's about seventy-eight degrees."

Chrisna frowned.

"Twenty-six Celsius," Zenelda said and stared at Chrisna for a long time.

"What?"

"Nothing."

As they pushed through the crowd, neither one of them gave way, and the people had to step around them.

"So where is this friend of yours?" Chrisna asked.

"He'll be at the festival, I'm sure of it."

Chrisna stopped. "This wasn't just a way for you to get me to go to the festival, was it?"

Zenelda grinned. "Well, yes and no. He is a rare coin collector. I met him at the festival the last time I was here. He had this amazing stand—"

"That was fifteen years ago." Chrisna gaped at her.

"Yes, but I've been back here a couple of times since

then. The last time I saw him was two years ago and he's still in the business. I'm almost certain that he'll be at the festival."

"You're *almost* certain?"

"You have a better idea of finding out what that coin means?"

Chrisna sighed. "No."

"Then just trust me."

They crossed a big intersection and Chrisna saw that the trees on either side of the street in front of them had been trimmed to look like squares. She stopped, lifted her sunglasses, and looked up at the beautiful, green-colored leaves.

"You okay?" Zenelda asked.

"Ja, I've just never seen such a beautiful shade of green before." She placed her glasses back over her eyes and took out the second bottle of water from her purse, drinking half of it.

"Thirsty?" Zenelda asked.

She swallowed. "My mouth's a little dry."

"I really think we should go back to your hotel room, just for a little while."

"Why?"

Zenelda looked at Chrisna for a few moments and then sighed. "Okay, but tell me where you're staying, just in case."

"In case of what?"

"It's just so I—"

"Ooh, wow. Look at that," Chrisna said and hurried

past her. Pushing through the crowd, she stopped when she reached a man juggling eight balls. She stared up at the colored balls swooshing through the air.

"Come on, we have to go," Zenelda said.

"In a minute."

"It's been almost five minutes."

"No, it hasn't. I just got here," Chrisna said and turned to Zenelda.

"We have to go." Zenelda took her by the elbow.

Chrisna pulled out of her grip. "Don't touch me. Stop grabbing my arm, it's really annoying."

"Okay." Zenelda stepped back. "But we really have to go."

Chrisna took another big sip of her water but there were only a few drops left. She looked at the juggler again, now lying on the ground while throwing the balls into the air. "Okay," she said, but when she took a step, her feet felt strange. She looked down at her black ballet pumps and took another few steps. Stopping, she lifted her foot and looked under the sole. Seeing nothing out of the ordinary, she lifted the other foot but couldn't see anything strange.

"What's wrong?" Zenelda asked.

"It feels like I'm walking on sponges," she said and raised the bottle of water to her mouth, but it was empty. She looked at her hand and tightened her grip on the bottle, her hand felt numb.

"Please let me take you back to your hotel," Zenelda said.

Chrisna suddenly felt feverish and her limbs felt swollen. "Okay," she said and swallowed a few times, her tongue feeling thick in her mouth.

She followed Zenelda down the sidewalk, stepping carefully as she tried to walk normally, but she struggled to feel the ground underneath her feet.

"I'll try and get us a cab," Zenelda said, and Chrisna looked at the cars standing bumper to bumper in the massive street. "We'll try the next intersection. How are you doing?"

Still clutching the water bottle in her hand, she raised it to her mouth but it was empty. "I'm thirsty," she said and her voice sounded deeper than usual. She swallowed again but she couldn't get the cotton ball feeling out of her mouth.

"There's a drinks stand just up ahead," Zenelda said. "Do you want a soda?"

Chrisna nodded, feeling too embarrassed to speak again. She didn't like the way her voice sounded. Slowing down, she stepped in behind Zenelda to avoid the people walking toward her, the ones passing too close by her, and those staring at her. The voices coming from the hordes of people on all sides resonated in her skull. She tried to breathe normally but her heart raced and pounded in her throat. She thought she heard Zenelda mumble something but she wasn't sure if she had, and she wanted to ask her what she'd said but she couldn't remember if she'd already done that. She stayed quiet and kept her eyes on Zenelda's red leather boots as she followed behind her.

The cool liquid felt good running down her throat and Chrisna swallowed as quickly as she could.

"How are you feeling?" Zenelda mumbled.

Chrisna looked at Zenelda and then looked around her. They were standing underneath the large branches of a tree and there were no sign of the stand. She couldn't remember them buying the drink or how they ended up where they were. Her chest tightened again and she stepped toward the tree, leaning her back against the trunk. The soda can fell out of her hand and she watched it slowly dropping to the ground, twice.

Zenelda opened the backdoor of a black car with a white sign on the roof, '*Taxi-Parisien*'. "Get in," she said, holding the door.

Chrisna looked from her to the car, to the cars swooshing past them. She looked down at the sidewalk, her head felt heavy.

"Get in," Zenelda said repeatedly until she looked up.

It was a lot of effort but she managed to shake her head.

"Can we try to get another cab now?" Zenelda mumbled.

Chrisna was lying on her back, staring up at the one small cloud hanging above her head. It looked like a puppy running away from something, probably something chasing him. But who was chasing him? What was chasing him?

"Sweetie?"

Something touched her hand and she pulled away. The sharp blades of the grass cut her skin as she moved her arms to try to sit up. It took a long time for her to sit up. "I want to walk. I have to walk," Chrisna said, her voice sounding even deeper as she pushed the words through her dry mouth, and stood up fast, very fast.

"There's another cab."

"I'm not getting in that car."

"I know where you're staying."

"We have to walk. I want to walk. Can we walk?"

"Where's your cell phone?"

"I should've given him my number."

"You did what? I'm so proud of you."

"I was running so fast."

"You'll be okay, I promise."

"We have to go down here."

"Too many people."

"I'm hungry."

"No, it's this way."

"You're going the wrong way."

"Weird sign."

"I can hear music. Am I supposed to hear music?"

"We're going to the hotel."

"Why?"

"What?"

"Who?"

"I'm hungry."

Six

Chrisna felt too embarrassed to open her eyes. She knew she was in her hotel room, lying on her back on the bed. She'd been awake for a while, recalling everything she could remember. Refusing to get into a taxi, insisting that she knew where her hotel was when she didn't, and making Zenelda walk all the way, even the four flights of stairs up to her room because she'd refused to get into the elevator.

She hoped that when she opened her eyes Zenelda wouldn't be there anymore, but the first thing she saw when she turned her head, was a blurry image of Zenelda, sitting on the couch, watching her.

"Are you feeling better?"

Chrisna pushed herself up. "Ja, I'm fine." Her throat scratched but her voice sounded normal again. Her head throbbed and she had a horrible taste in her mouth. She sat upright, pushing the tips of her index fingers against her temples and closing her eyes again, shielding them from the bright light streaming in through the window.

"Here," Zenelda said, and when Chrisna opened her eyes again, Zenelda was standing beside the bed, holding a glass of water and a white paper sachet. "I found this in your purse."

Chrisna took the sachet from her, tore it open, and then sprinkled the white powder on her tongue before taking the glass and sipping on the water. Placing the glass on the nightstand, she saw her glasses and picked them up, pushing them onto her nose. She looked at her watch, 8.13pm. "How long was I asleep?"

"Only a couple of hours," Zenelda said and grinned. "It took us a while to get here."

"I'm sorry," Chrisna said and glanced at the two pizza boxes on the desk. "I ate that?"

"You were starving."

"How much did I eat?" Chrisna asked, surprised that she didn't feel full.

Zenelda sat down on the couch again and leaned forward. "About a pie and a half before you threw up."

Stunned, Chrisna glanced around the room and then sighed with relief when she couldn't see any throw-up on the carpet. "I don't even like pizza."

"Boom!"

Chrisna shut her eyes.

"Sorry," Zenelda whispered. "But you don't like pizza?"

"No."

"It didn't seem that way earlier. You insisted that you wanted pizza with extra cheese."

Chrisna felt queasy when she thought about biting into the thick warm greasy cheese. "No wonder I threw up."

Zenelda grinned. "I don't think it was just from the pizza."

Chrisna moved her legs over the side of the bed and stood up, stretching her back. "I don't think I like your friend very much."

"Well, I'm not too fond of him either at the moment," Zenelda said and stood up. "I'm really sorry about what happened."

Zenelda's eyes were big and sincere and Chrisna forced a grin. "It's okay. It wasn't your fault."

"I better get going," Zenelda said. "I just stayed to see that you were okay."

"Is it too late to try to find your friend with the coins?"

Zenelda looked surprised. "No, the festival runs the entire weekend, so we can go tomorrow if you want."

"I have a lot to do tomorrow," Chrisna said. "What time do they close tonight?"

"The stands probably close around twelve, but are you sure you're up for it?"

Her headache was already subsiding. "Sure, I've had stomach viruses worse than this," she said. "Besides, I'm hungry and I'm not eating the pizza. Just give me a second to freshen up, change, and brush my teeth."

It had taken about fifteen minutes for them to walk to Café 6Two on Rue Cambon.

Sitting outside under a yellow awning at a wooden high top table, Chrisna looked through the large window into the café. The waiters, dressed all in white, moved around quickly, serving the packed room with its amber-cone ceiling pendants hanging above every table. It was just before 9pm and it was still light out. She could hear music in the distance, a deep bass beat resonating in their direction. The street in front of the café was very narrow, just wide enough for the passing vehicles to squeeze past the parked cars and scooters on the side of the road. She glanced at the large solid-wood doors in the gray four-storey building across the street, and then looked to her right at the only two other tables next to theirs on the sidewalk. An elderly couple sat at the table farthest from the entrance, and they didn't seem at all interested in talking to each other as they stared out in front of them, every now and again taking a sip of their coffee. At the middle table, a young couple sat arm in arm, fawning over each other, oblivious to everything else going on around them.

Just before they'd left her hotel room, Chrisna had changed into a blue camisole and a white three-quarter sleeve top with tiny blue flowers that fastened with a string just below her breasts. She still wore her black jeans, but had swapped her ballet pumps for her trainers, and she'd tied her hair back into a high ponytail.

"You *have* to order a Crêpe," Zenelda said from behind her menu.

Chrisna glanced at the selection on her menu. She

skipped the breakfast section and looked farther down. There were savory Crêpes with cream cheese and spinach, Crêpes filled with chopped ham, stir-fry, or asparagus topped with a Hollandaise sauce. The selection sounded a little too heavy, so she looked at the dessert range. Crêpes filled with sweetened ricotta cheese, or ice cream with chopped nuts and whipped cream…

"The chocolate sauce they make here is to die for," Zenelda said and peered over her menu.

"Please don't say '*boom*' again, but I don't really like chocolate," Chrisna said, and she could see Zenelda struggling to hold back her surprise. "I can eat a little bit every once in a while but it's too sweet. I'm not a big fan of sweet things."

The waiter brought their drinks; a small black coffee for Chrisna and a tall caramel iced coffee for Zenelda, and took their food order. Zenelda enthusiastically ordered a Crêpe with chocolate sauce but Chrisna opted for one with a seasonal fruit mix, no ice cream.

The waiter took their menus and left.

"So," Chrisna said, "you were telling me about your record store."

"Oh, yes. It's a small place in Camden, cozy actually, and I don't sell CD's, they sound too clean. Vinyl's the only way to go." She sipped her iced coffee through the straw. "My favorite part of the store is the room I constructed in the back, kinda like a lounge area where artists come and perform every Thursday night. On Fridays we have an open mic night."

"Do you sing?" Chrisna asked and took a sip of her coffee.

"Frequently and loudly but not very well." Zenelda smiled. "I love to karaoke though. Have you ever tried it?"

"Karaoke?" Chrisna smirked. "No, but I did sing in the elevator at the Eiffel Tower."

"Close the gates. You did what?"

"The door was stuck and people started to panic. This guy started singing, so I sang along, everyone did."

Zenelda grinned. "So you hugged the Venus de Milo and you sung in front of a crowd. Color me crazy but I think that's two ticks off your list."

"You know about the Venus de Milo?"

"Yeah, you told me," Zenelda said, "this afternoon, when we passed by the Louvre. I think your exact words were '*the statue hugged me*'."

Chrisna blushed. "Guess I was pretty out of it." She took another sip of her coffee. "But I don't think my singing in the elevator counts. You said I had to sing in front of a crowd of at least fifty people and there were only about twenty other people on the elevator."

Zenelda smiled. "Do details bother you?"

Chrisna frowned. "That's a strange question."

"Do strange questions bother you?"

She looked at Zenelda, not knowing how to answer.

"I'm messing with you," Zenelda said.

"You have a weird sense of humor."

"You're just weird, period."

"Why do you say that?" Chrisna asked and twirled the end of her ponytail between her fingers.

"You came all this way to Paris to throw your ring off the Eiffel Tower," Zenelda said, taking a long sip of her iced coffee. "And then you don't. And don't tell me it's because you had to meet up with me."

Chrisna looked down at her hands and whispered, "Not doing something doesn't make me weird."

"No, I guess not. But weird's not an insult, sweetie. Well, not when it's coming from me," Zenelda said. "What's your husband like?"

"Ex-husband." Chrisna looked at her.

"Okay, fine. Ex-husband. Tell me what he's like."

"Werner's a good guy."

"I've met many good guys in my day. It don't mean squat. Why did you get divorced?"

Chrisna looked down again and twirled her cup on the saucer. "We met in Primary School. We dated in High School. We were engaged in college and we got married shortly after that. Everyone said we were the perfect couple."

"But you weren't."

"I guess not." She looked up again. "We were friends, great friends, but all we knew were *us*. I only knew *him*."

Zenelda sat back in her chair, folded her arms, and looked at Chrisna for a long time. "You can marry your friend but all you are then, is married to a friend."

Chrisna gaped at Zenelda. "That's it exactly."

Zenelda smiled, placed her lips over the straw, and sipped.

"He worked on his dad's potato farm after college. We lived with his parents for a while until we could build our own little place on their farm. But it was all so generic. Get a degree, get a job, get a house, have children. I'm just glad we didn't."

"Have children?" Zenelda asked.

"Ja."

"Do you want children?"

"I don't know."

Zenelda frowned. "That's not an answer. Either you do or you don't."

"If I do someday, great. If I don't, that's fine too. How about you?"

Zenelda looked at her glass as she took another sip from the straw. "I almost had a kid once."

Chrisna's eyes widened. "What do you mean?"

Zenelda remained quiet for a while before she answered. "I'd just broken out on my own." She glimpsed at Chrisna but then looked at her glass again as she took another sip. "I was barely nineteen. I wasn't ready. I was too young. So I let her go."

"Her?"

"It was a girl. They told me it was too soon to tell, but I knew." Zenelda looked up, and Chrisna saw the hurt in her eyes for a second before she shrugged it off and forced a grin. "Joe never wanted kids, so we didn't."

"So if you're here in Paris for your, what did you call

it, marital sabbatical…?

Zenelda forced a smile. "Yes."

"Then where's your husband?"

The waiter brought their food.

"Wow, the fruit looks delicious," Zenelda said as she took a bite of her chocolate Crêpe. "Did you always want to be a teacher?"

"Both my parents are lectors at the University of the Free State. That's where they met. My dad's a professor of Theology and my mom teaches Economics," Chrisna said and took a bite. The fruit had a crisp sweet and sour taste and she liked it.

"So tell me," Zenelda said. "What did you really want to do with your life?"

Chrisna frowned. "What do you mean? I just told you—"

"That your parents are teachers. Yeah, I got that."

Chrisna sighed. "Well, there was a time when I considered studying music. I can play the piano and a little bit of guitar."

"You should've done that." Zenelda smiled. "To me, music is the ultimate form of expression. It's so intimate."

"Intimate," Chrisna repeated and she suddenly had a lump in her throat.

"May I ask why you actually got divorced?" Zenelda asked, almost whispering.

Chrisna twirled her wedding ring around her finger again. "It wasn't anything specific. It took a long time for us to drift apart. I think it started when we stopped talking about the little things, like how our day was. We stopped putting in effort to spend time together. Life became a routine; work, dinner, bed. He would be out of the house before I woke up and go to bed while I was still preparing my lessons for the following day. We started to live past each other, I think." She took a sip of her coffee. "Kissing became a peck on the cheek before work, after work, and before he went to bed." She looked up at Zenelda. "We even stopped fighting."

Zenelda frowned. "Joe and I fought about everything." She cleared her throat. "We're both very passionate people but every fight always ends with, '*You drive me crazy*'." She smiled. "That's our way of saying, '*I love you*', and then we'll have the most amazing makeup-sex, of course."

"Of course." Chrisna grinned and looked down at her ring again. "I haven't had sex in four years." She blushed, unable to believe what she'd just admitted.

"Boom!"

Chrisna jumped in her seat and looked at Zenelda, who gaped at her.

"When did you get divorced again?"

"Just over a month ago."

"And you haven't been with anyone since then?"

"No." Chrisna twirled the end of her ponytail again. "I've actually never been with anyone but Werner."

"Atomic boom," Zenelda said, softer this time, and gave her a sympathetic look.

"It's not a big deal."

"Aw, sweetie." Zenelda touched Chrisna's hand. "No wonder you're still not over him."

"I *am* over him," Chrisna said, unintentionally raising her voice.

"Then why do you still wear that ring?"

Chrisna pulled her hand away and looked at the ring again.

"And what made you decide to get rid of it in such a dramatic way?"

Chrisna looked at her. "I was angry when I made that comment. Sandra had just told me that she'd seen Werner with another woman, some woman that works at the bank." She suddenly felt angry. "He should've told me he was dating."

"You miss him."

"No, I don't." She raised her voice again.

Zenelda took the last bite of her Crêpe and chewed on it for a long time while watching Chrisna.

Chrisna stared at the half-eaten Crêpe and pushed the pieces of fruit around with her fork. "Sometimes," she said and placed the fork on her plate before checking the time, 9.42pm. "I think we should go."

"Okay," Zenelda said. "But can I have a taste of your Crêpe? I've never had one with fruit before."

"Sure," Chrisna said and pushed her plate forward.

Zenelda reached over and bumped her hand against the tall glass of iced coffee. It fell over and splashed coffee onto Chrisna's top.

She flinched, stood up, and stepped away from the table, watching as the brown liquid dripped off the edge.

Zenelda forced a grin. "Sorry."

Chrisna looked down at the white top with the blue flowers and the brown stain over her left side.

Zenelda reached down, picked up Chrisna's purse from the ground between their chairs, and held it up. "Wet wipes," she said, still grinning.

Chrisna stepped forward, took the purse and placed it on her chair. Taking out the packet of wipes, she frowned as she carefully wiped the excess coffee from her top and jeans. Luckily, her jeans were black, so the stain wasn't visible, but the top was ruined.

"I think it's ruined," Zenelda said, reading her mind.

Chrisna grinned. "You think so?"

"Sorry."

Removing her top, she hung it over the back of her chair and continued to rub the stain. "We'll have to go back to my hotel room," she said, giving up. "I'm not going to the festival wearing *only* this." She pointed to the blue camisole she had on underneath the white top.

"Why not? You look good."

Frowning, Chrisna looked down at the material stretching over her stomach, and she pulled on the hem. "It's too tight."

"What are you talking about? You have a great body. Do you work out?"

Chrisna blushed, looked up and then grinned. "Are you hitting on me?"

Zenelda laughed loudly and then snorted. "No, seriously, you look fine. You have nothing to be ashamed of." She quickly glanced over Chrisna's body. "Trust me. Nothing."

Feeling her cheeks burning, Chrisna pulled the camisole as far down over her hips as it would go, and then she rolled the white top into a small ball and pushed it into her purse. She sighed, looked at Zenelda, and said, "Okay, I trust you."

Seven

Feeling a little self-conscious, Chrisna kept her arms folded over her chest as they walked in a south-easterly direction down Rue Cambon. It was getting dark fast, and she shivered when a cool breeze blew against her neck. The closer they came to Place de la Concorde, the louder the music became, and the more she could feel the bass beating in her chest. It was becoming increasingly difficult to move through the hordes of people occupying the sidewalk, and she pushed the strap of her purse farther up her shoulder and turned the bag so it covered her chest.

They turned right on Rue Saint-Honoré and walked against the congested traffic. There was less and less room to move as the people pushed against one another to get to their destinations. Passing a few designer clothing stores, Chrisna peaked in through the windows at the beautiful outfits, and then briefly glanced down at her plain blue camisole, before someone bumped into her again and she had to concentrate on getting through the crowd.

About five minutes later, they turned left on Rue

Saint-Florentin and had to queue to squeeze through a narrow gate in the security barrier.

When Chrisna finally looked up, she gaped at the thousands upon thousands of blue fairy lights suspended between the lampposts on both sides of the street.

Chrisna jumped when a ball of fire exploded in the air in front of her as she entered through the gate.

"Fire blowers. They'll get you every time," Zenelda laughed, as Chrisna stole a glance at the skinny, shirtless man taking another sip of something from a clear bottle.

Stands were lined up on the left side of the street, and they paused beside each one to look at the goods, but none of them displayed any coins.

They stopped at the next stand where a bulgy tattooed man with a shaved head, sat at a table drawing a Humming Bird on the shoulder of an even bulgier man.

"Want one?" Zenelda grinned.

Chrisna smiled. "A Humming Bird? No."

"I think I already know the answer, but do you have any tattoos?"

"Do you?"

Zenelda turned to Chrisna and lifted her shirt, pointing to a sun around her bellybutton. "This was my first one," she said. "I got it the day after I arrived in LA." Turning slightly, she lifted her shirt higher up and pulled down her belt a fraction so Chrisna could see a swallow tattooed on her hip. "I love this one. It symbolizes freedom." She pulled her shirt back down, turned her back to Chrisna, lifted her hair, and revealed a tiny star on the nape of her neck. "I got this one at Woodstock '94."

"Love your ink," the tattoo artist said.

Zenelda smiled, let go of her hair, and turned to Chrisna again. "Then I have a small butterfly on my big toe," she pointed to her left foot, "A dream catcher around my right ankle and a *'tramp stamp'* just above my—"

"A tramp stamp?" Chrisna frowned.

"Yes. It literally looks like a stamp that says *'tramp'*." She smiled. "I was a little intoxicated when I got it last year."

Chrisna smiled.

"So *do* you have one?" Zenelda asked.

Chrisna grinned. "If you're so sure that I don't, why do you ask?"

"Because you've been able to surprise me a couple of times with your weird dislike of normal things, like pizza, chocolate, beer, ice cream—"

"And milk," Chrisna interrupted her.

"Boom!" Zenelda shouted incredulously and threw her arms in the air. "See?" She lowered her arms and touched Chrisna's shoulder. "I never thought you would actually hug the Venus de Milo either."

"I even surprised myself with that one."

"So do you have a tattoo?" Zenelda asked dutifully and waited with obvious anticipation for Chrisna to answer.

"Not yet." Chrisna smiled and walked on.

"Not yet? What does that mean? Do you want to get

one? What would you get?" Zenelda rambled on about butterflies, hearts, and band logos, and came to a sudden halt as she bumped into Chrisna, who suddenly stopped.

A mime had stepped in front of her, dressed in a black and white striped shirt, with black suspenders holding up his long black pants. His white face looked frozen as he stood with his left arm propped up as if he was holding onto a bag, just as Chrisna was. His right arm hung next to his side and his left foot was a few inches in front of his right, mirroring her.

Chrisna remembered that one of her tasks on the list Zenelda gave her, was to get a mime to speak, so she said, "Hello." But the mime didn't reply. He merely stared at her with an eerie expression that made her uncomfortable. "Hello," she said again, but when his expression didn't change, she took a step to her right to try to walk around him, but he stepped left and blocked her way again. She pushed her glasses up on her nose and he imitated the action. She glanced at Zenelda, who looked amused.

Looking back at the mime, Chrisna shook her head, and when he did the same, she sprinted around him and jogged down the street.

He quickly caught up to her, and she slowed down to a brisk walk. Walking alongside her, he copied her quick steps. She walked even faster, and he walked faster. She stopped, and he stopped. She glanced at Zenelda, who had caught up to her again.

"Don't do it," Zenelda said and grinned.

Chrisna frowned and then sprinted off, running as fast as she could. When she looked behind her, the mime was gone. She slowed down, but just as she looked in front of her again, she crashed into a long wooden pole.

Surprised that the pole moved, she looked up as it tipped over. On top of the ten foot pole, stood a man dressed in red, and she heard someone shriek as he jumped to the ground, landing next to her as his stilts fell down.

"Is jy okay?" Chrisna asked shocked and hurried to help him up, but before she could, he pushed himself off the ground, and the onlookers started clapping.

"I'm so sorry," she said as she watched the man dust himself off, mumble something she didn't understand, and then give her a look that is universally understood.

He walked to where his stilts were, and Chrisna shouted, "I *am* sorry!", but he didn't turn around.

"Nice going," Zenelda said when she stopped beside her.

Chrisna forced a grin. "Is tackling a stilt-walker on your list?"

"No." Zenelda snickered. "But it should be."

"Come on," Chrisna giggled, and they continued down the street, stopping a few times to look at some of the other stands.

Zenelda lingered for a while at a homemade jewelry display and when they left, they had reached the end of the street.

Chrisna gaped at the enormous crowd in front of

her. She had never seen so many people in her life. There had to be at least a few hundred thousand people filling the space between them and a massive stage, towering over the hordes on the other side of Place de la Concorde. The music blared as a band performed under the colorful roaming lights.

"I guess your friend's not here," Chrisna said and felt a little disappointed.

"What?!" Zenelda shouted.

Chrisna leaned in closer to her. "Your friend! Coins! Not here!"

Zenelda grinned. "Come on." She took her hand and forced her to follow as they walked on the outside of a building with numerous brick arches.

They turned right into Rue Royale, a bigger street with even more visitors, and even more stands. There were stands with flags of the world, chocolate, and kitchen utensils, but no coins. They checked each stand and Zenelda spent more time at the vintage toy display, looking at the tea sets, spinning tops, and cap guns.

When they reached the intersection, Chrisna saw a large building that looked like a Greek temple with its massive columns, and they turned left, hurried down the busy sidewalk, and turned left again into Rue Boissy-d'Anglas. This time the fairy lights were red.

They passed a few jugglers, acrobats, and another flame blower, and then Zenelda stopped.

"What is it?" Chrisna asked.

"Leverette!" Zenelda shouted and ran to a small

stand, stepping around a table, and hugging a plump man in a white dress shirt and brown slacks.

When Chrisna neared the stand, she saw a large selection of coins in various sizes in a display case on the metal table. Next to it, was a metal jewelry stand with coins hanging from silver and gold chains.

"Those are popular with the younger crowd," the man said when Chrisna touched one of the necklaces.

"This is Leverette," Zenelda said, smiling broadly.

Chrisna stretched her arm out over the table and shook the man's hand.

His chubby cheeks pushed up to his eyes when he smiled a pleasant smile.

"Chrisna," she said, and Zenelda frowned at her.

"How have you been, child?" Leverette asked Zenelda.

He couldn't have been more than ten years older than Zenelda but the way he spoke made him sound like her grandfather.

"I'm great, thanks," Zenelda said. "Back in good ol' Paree."

"How's Joe? Still writing those beautiful songs?" he asked.

The necklace stand clunked onto the metal tabletop as it fell over, and Chrisna quickly pulled her hand back when Leverette and Zenelda looked at her.

Picking it up, she tried to redo the display.

"Don't worry about it, child," Leverette said.

"Skees," Chrisna said, pushed her glasses up on the

bridge of her nose, and stepped back, allowing him to place the necklaces in their original positions.

"Clumsy over there has something she'd like to show you," Zenelda said and smiled.

"Ja." Chrisna reached into her purse and pulled out the silver coin.

When Leverette finished the display, Chrisna handed him the coin. "Where are you from?" he asked.

"South Africa."

"Ah, home of the Krugerrand," Leverette said as he examined the coin.

"Ja," Chrisna said. "My dad actually has five. He keeps them in his safe because they're worth something like—"

"A thousand Euros each," he interrupted her.

"Boom!" Zenelda said, and both Chrisna and Leverette jumped.

"You're still doing that I see." Leverette frowned. "You're going to give someone a heart attack someday."

Zenelda's smile instantly faded.

"You see this here." Leverette pointed to the eight-point star on the one side of the silver coin. "This symbol appears in cultures around the world. It can be found in religious iconography, as well as on national flags, but the meaning is different with each culture that uses it. There are eight paths in the way of the Buddha and eight immortals in Chinese tradition, but the universal symbolism is balance, harmony, and cosmic order. It can be associated with early astronomy and mysticism."

Chrisna listened attentively.

"The eight-point star is the star of redemption or regeneration," Leverette continued as he flipped the coined over. "These three flowers, on the other hand, look like daisies to me."

"I also thought so," Chrisna said.

"A daisy," Leverette continued, "is a symbol of purity, innocence, beauty, patience, loyal love, and simplicity, and it's also the sacred symbol of the Virgin Mary, signifying her chastity." He smiled. "Then there's the famous phrase, '*Fresh as a Daisy*', of course. I have to admit, I've never seen a coin like this before. It looks like it's been custom-made within the last decade or so." He smiled and handed the coin back to Chrisna. "But I'm only guessing."

"Is it worth anything?" Zenelda asked intrigued.

He moved his hand up and down as if weighing the coin. "Well, it's silver, so it should be worth at least a few dozen Euros." He looked at Chrisna again. "Where did you get it?"

"That's what we're trying to figure out," Zenelda answered for her.

"I'm sorry I can't be of more help," Leverette said.

Chrisna looked at the coin one more time, sighed, and then pushed it back into her purse. "Thank you."

"Ooh," Zenelda said. "I love this song." She turned to Leverette, gave him a tight hug, and then kissed him on the cheek. "Thanks."

He grinned shyly and his chubby cheeks instantly

turned red.

"Come on." Zenelda rushed around the table and grabbed Chrisna's hand.

"Thank you!" Chrisna yelled as Zenelda pulled her away. "Where are we going?"

Moments later, they stepped into the enormous crowd of people dancing, clapping, and jumping to the rhythm of a rock song.

"Amazing, isn't it?" Zenelda shouted as she pulled Chrisna in the direction of the stage. She glanced back. "We have to get closer!" she yelled. "I know this band."

Chrisna didn't know the song but the people she pushed against seemed to enjoy it as they animatedly sang along.

They passed a large round fountain with black and green mermaids, holding golden fishes. People were sitting and standing on the edge, some danced in the water, and others had climbed onto the middle disc, raising them over the crowd. Halfway to the stage, Chrisna looked up at the obelisk on her right, towering over them, and her hand slipped out of Zenelda's. She struggled to keep up, and caught a glimpse of her once more before she disappeared.

Chrisna pushed forward. "Skees," she said every time she passed someone who wasn't happy about letting her go by. "Skees," she said every time she stepped on someone's foot or was pushed into them. Eventually she stopped saying 'skees', pulled her shoulders back, and forced her way through the crowd.

She passed an exact replica of the previous fountain, and the band was in the middle of their fourth song when she finally made it to the front. She looked around but there were too many people, women especially, standing against the guardrails that stood about three meters from the stage.

The women shrieked, cheered, and bounced to the rhythm of the song. The music was too loud, and Chrisna wouldn't have been able to hear or call for Zenelda as she was stuck in the mass near the middle of the stage.

Looking up, she turned cold when she saw the guy playing the electric guitar. Tyce.

Dressed in white trainers, blue jeans, and a bright red t-shirt, his fingers glided over the strings of his metallic black guitar, and Chrisna couldn't help but admit to herself that he looked extremely sexy.

She watched only him for the next two songs, and as he played the last chord, she could've sworn he looked directly at her and smiled. Her heart jumped into her throat and she knew she was blushing. She smiled back at him, but so did the dozens of girls surrounding her.

Shrugging off her disappointment, she watched him walk to the middle of the stage and whisper something in the lead singer's ear. The singer smiled, nodded, and then stretched his arm out in the air and pointed at Tyce, who struck a chord.

The crowd cheered as he approached the microphone. "I'd like to sing you a song," he said and his voice echoed over the screaming girls. "I wrote this a while ago." He pulled his guitar strap off his shoulders, and a man dressed in black, handed him a high stool and an acoustic guitar. As he placed the strap over his head, he said, "I met a girl the other night and she reminded me of what this song is really about." The crowd cheered. "It's called '*Trying on the World*.'"

Tyce picked the strings, and Chrisna's heart pounded against her chest. She knew he couldn't have been talking about her. He's a musician and a popular one by the looks of it. He must have his pick of swooning girls. No, he wasn't talking about her.

She listened as he started to sing, and she loved the tone of his voice. Just like his laugh, his voice was warm when he sang.

The drone of the crowd faded away, and Tyce might as well have been singing to only her as she listened to the chorus. "*Life knocks you over, but it's worth the hit. You may not see it, but it's not over yet. The way you want it, may not always fit. But you're only trying on the world.*"

He ended the song by strumming the strings in a downward motion, and Chrisna looked intently at him as the sound of the cheering crowd gradually resurfaced.

"Thank you," he said, bowed his head for a second, and when he looked up, he smiled, and she knew that time he was smiling at her.

The band played one more song before leaving the stage and a DJ took over.

Chrisna pushed through the crowd to the right side of the stage.

"There you are!" Zenelda yelled and rushed over to her.

"What?!" Chrisna shouted and cupped her ear as the beat resonated through her body. "Can we go somewhere quieter?"

"What?!"

She waved Zenelda away from the stage and stopped where the guardrails formed a corner.

Two large men, dressed in black, stood arms folded in front of a gate in the barricade. Chrisna stopped and turned to Zenelda. "I want to go back stage," she said.

"Boom!" Zenelda shouted. "We don't have passes, but I'm sure we can figure something out."

"You're not going to ask me why?"

"Do you want me to?"

Chrisna shook her head. "Not really."

"Alright then." Zenelda smiled. "Conventional way first," she said, took off her newsboy cap, handed it to Chrisna, ruffled her hair, pushed her breasts up, and walked over to the guards in black. "Hi," she said, flicking her hair, but they stared straight ahead, not acknowledging her, and she returned to where Chrisna stood. Taking her hat, she pushed it back onto her head. "They must not like redheads. Okay, plan B. Untie your hair, take off your glasses, and pull up that camisole. You'll need to show some skin." Zenelda took Chrisna's purse, flung the strap over her shoulder, reached down, and pulled on the hem of her camisole.

Grabbing her hands, Chrisna pushed them away and

stepped back. "No."

Zenelda sighed. "Have it your way, but for plan C we'll need a pair of pliers, some baby powder, super glue, and a sixty-four piece puzzle."

Chrisna frowned and then smiled. "Okay, that was funny."

Zenelda frowned. "It wasn't a joke."

"Anyway," Chrisna said, "I think I'd like to try something." She took her purse from Zenelda and walked over to the guards, said something to one of them, and he touched his ear before speaking into his sleeve.

About two minutes later, he opened the gate, and Chrisna looked back at Zenelda, waving her over.

Zenelda's jaw dropped and she hurried after Chrisna, who stepped through the gate. "Still surprising me," she said as she fell in beside her.

Chrisna smiled as the guard pointed in the direction they should go.

Heading through the narrow pathway next to a high chain-linked fence, they walked past the side of the stage, and around the outside where at least seven large trailers stood back to back. Crew members in shirts with '*Mise en Scène*' printed on the back, carried around cables, ladders, and musical instruments.

"So, what did you say to him?" Zenelda asked.

Chrisna smiled. "I showed him the coin."

Zenelda gaped at her. "And that worked?"

"No, but when I told him my name was Kristal, he—"

"You did what?"

"What?" Chrisna couldn't help but grin. "I'm going to try on this Kristal-thing."

Zenelda smiled, almost proudly. "So how did Kristal convince him to let us in?"

She smiled. "Remember that guy I went to the party with? The party I can't remember—"

"Please wait here," another guard said, and stopped them when they'd reached the end of the fence.

"It's okay, she's with me." Tyce walked up from behind the guard. "Hi," he said to Chrisna, grinning shyly.

She blushed. "Hi."

He'd change into a white t-shirt that accentuated his toned arms.

"Tyce?" Zenelda said, and his eyes widened.

Chrisna watched the two of them, who seemed extremely uncomfortable.

Tyce looked from Zenelda to Chrisna and back again. "Wow." He rubbed the back of his neck. "Zenelda, I didn't expect to see you here."

"Tyce is the guy?" She gaped at Chrisna, who glared at her, and she cleared her throat. "Who you went to the party with?"

Chrisna smiled shyly, nodded, and fidgeted with the end of her ponytail.

For a long awkward second, there was silence as Zenelda glanced from Chrisna to Tyce.

"You'll need these," Tyce finally said. He pulled two backstage passes from the back pocket of his jeans, gave one to Zenelda and when he handed Chrisna hers, his fingers touched her palm and a cold shiver ran down her spine. He smiled his perfect smile.

Chrisna blushed and quickly pulled the string over her head, letting the laminated paper dangle against her stomach.

"Follow me," he said and walked out in front toward one of the large trailers.

"How do you know Tyce?" Chrisna asked quietly while still trying to talk over the music.

Zenelda forced a grin and pulled the string over her head. "He used to play at the open mic nights at my store."

Tyce stopped in front of the trailer and opened the door with a banner above it, reading 'Solid Flint'. "After you," he said, and Zenelda hurried in.

Chrisna glanced at Tyce when she passed him and ascended two of the small steps, but her toes hit the third one and she stumbled forward.

Tyce grabbed her around her waist and pulled her back. "Careful," he said.

Feeling her skin heat up where his hands touched her body, all she could utter was, "Thank you," before pulling out of his hold and stepping into the trailer.

She walked past a mini fridge and saw two long black couches standing against either side of the trailer's light-blue walls, with beer bottles, glasses, and soda cans on the floor between them. At the back, a door partially obscured a small area, and she could see a bed through the opening. Next to one of the couches stood the acoustic guitar that Tyce had used to play his song, her song.

Zenelda had already made herself comfortable on the couch on the right and were flipping through a magazine.

"Sorry about the mess," Tyce said, rubbing the back of his neck. "Would you like something to drink?" he asked Chrisna.

"I'll take a beer," Zenelda said without looking up.

Tyce looked at Chrisna. "A beer will be fine, thanks," she said and twirled the end of her ponytail again.

"Two beers, coming up. Have a seat." Tyce opened the fridge.

Chrisna quickly walked over to where Zenelda sat, but when she tried to sit down, Zenelda glared at her, stretched her body to take up most of the space, and shook her head.

"What?" Chrisna mouthed.

"Sit there," Zenelda mouthed back and pointed to the other couch.

"No."

"Yes."

Tyce turned around with three bottles of beer in his hands, and Chrisna quickly sat down on the other couch, placing her purse next to her on the black leather cushion.

"Here you go," he said, handing Zenelda one of the beers, and then he sat down next to Chrisna's purse and handed her one of the other bottles.

"Thank you," she said shyly as she took the cold bottle from him.

The silence continued for a little while, and Chrisna had never wished so hard that Zenelda would say something, anything, but she didn't. She looked down at the open bottle and restrained herself from wiping the top. Taking a sip, she forced back a cringe.

Tyce took a long sip of his beer, and then the door swung open.

"Dinner is served," the lead singer said in a British accent as he stepped into the trailer with two paper bags in hand. He was boyishly handsome with his short spiky dark hair. He stopped and looked from Zenelda to Chrisna.

"Hey! What gives?" the drummer asked when he bumped into the singer.

The drummer had a shaved head with a long beard, and he was much bigger than the other two band members were. Tattoos covered both his arms from wrist to shoulder.

Tyce jumped up. "Hey guys. This is Zenelda and Kristal," he said, pointing to them individually, and then he pointed to the singer. "This is Bran, as in the cereal." He smiled and the singer gave him a look. "And this is Jax."

The drummer smiled. "As in Jax you up." He walked over to Chrisna and shook her hand. "Nice to meet you," he said, also in a British accent, and turned to Zenelda, who jumped up and gave him a hug.

"Your beats are sick," Zenelda said before sitting down again.

Jax smiled. "Thanks babe," he said and sat down next to her.

Putting the paper bags down on the small table next to the fridge, Bran picked up a half-empty beer bottle from the floor, took a sip and sat down in Tyce's spot. "So we're having a party?" he asked and grinned.

Although he had a somewhat cute grin that curled up at the left side of his mouth, Chrisna didn't like it for some reason. She held her purse in place between them and shifted away a few inches.

Tyce took another long sip of his beer, walked past the couch and sat down on the other side of Chrisna, in a much smaller space. His leg touched hers and her body numbed.

"So, you girls liked our set?" Bran asked, looking directly at Chrisna.

She took a long sip of her beer.

"You guys were great," Zenelda answered. "But then I always knew Tyce was good."

Bran turned to face Zenelda. "Yeah?" He sounded a little offended.

Tyce shifted forward on the couch and his leg brushed against Chrisna's. "I've known Zenelda for years. I used to play at her open mic nights in Camden."

"Oh yeah?" Jax asked. "What's the place called?"

Zenelda grinned. "*Hot Vinyl.*"

"Oh yes," Jax said. "I've been in there a couple of

times. Great store."

"Thanks," Zenelda said and took a sip of her beer. "You wanna sign my shirt?"

"Sure." Jax glanced around the room, and then Tyce reached down next to the couch before tossing him a black marker. Catching it, he took off the cap with his teeth. "Where do you want it?' he mumbled.

Zenelda sat up straight and pulled down her shirt. "Here," she said, pointing at the material just above her breasts.

Jax smiled and scribbled an almost illegible signature across her chest.

"You want me to sign *your* shirt?" Bran asked Chrisna and grinned mischievously.

"No, thanks," she said and pushed her glasses up on the bridge of her nose.

"You can sign mine," Zenelda said, taking the marker from Jax and standing up.

Bran sighed. "Okay." He stood up, and Zenelda turned her back on him before slightly bending over. "There you go," he said when he had finished signing on the back of her shirt. He tossed the marker to Tyce, who caught it, and then he placed Chrisna's purse on the floor before sitting against her.

Turning back, Zenelda looked at Chrisna, who couldn't hide that she felt extremely uncomfortable. "Come on guys," Zenelda said. "I saw *Shreddings'* trailer when we came in, and they're always up for a few rounds."

"Sure," Jax said and stood up, but Bran lingered.

Zenelda leaned over and took his hand. "Come on." She pulled him to his feet.

Glancing back at Chrisna and Tyce, Bran sighed. "Fine," he said. "I don't think she'll put out anyway."

Chrisna gaped at Bran as he followed Zenelda and Jax out the door.

"I'm sorry about my friend," Tyce said when the door closed. "He can be a real ass when he wants to be."

Still sitting against Tyce, Chrisna couldn't force herself to look at him. She shifted a few inches to her right, creating a small gap between them.

"You want another drink?" he asked.

Looking at the half-full bottle in her hand, she downed the rest of the beer and then said, "Yes," knowing he'd have to get up, and as soon as he did, she moved to the middle of the couch.

Taking another beer from the fridge, Tyce turned around, handed her the drink, and stepped back, leaning against the small table.

Relieved, Chrisna placed the empty bottle near her feet on the floor and took a sip from the new one. "What happened between you and Zenelda?" she asked.

He frowned. "What do you mean?"

"Well, you seem a little uncomfortable around her."

Tyce rubbed the back of his neck again. "Let's just say, she knew me before I grew up." He forced a smile. "You know how they say that you're supposed to make mistakes in your twenties? Well, I think I took it a little too seriously."

Chrisna sipped from her beer and thought about the last decade she'd spent playing house. She pushed her glasses up on her nose.

"I'm glad you found me," Tyce said, and his stare burned into her.

She twirled her fingers around her ponytail as her cheeks heated up. "Is this what you meant when you said you're a musician *sometimes*?"

He grinned. "I do other things as well."

"Like what?"

"Well, I love extreme sports like bungee jumping, rock climbing, hang gliding, and there's my bike of course."

"You have a motorcycle?" Chrisna asked.

He frowned. "Yes. You don't remember? I showed it to you."

She frowned.

Smiling, Tyce took his cell phone out of his jeans' front pocket and sat down next to her. He ran his finger over the screen a few times and then pointed to a picture of a metallic black motorcycle. "It was parked outside La Fosse." He looked at her. "Where we met. But you refused to get on it. I think you called it '*a casket on wheels*'."

"So that's why we walked?" she asked.

He nodded.

"Skees."

He smiled and Chrisna looked down at his phone

again. "Sorry about all the trouble. You should've just left me there," she said.

"Probably." He locked the phone and returned it to his pocket. "And I probably shouldn't have let you kiss me either."

"What?" Her heart jumped into her throat and she looked up at him.

He whispered, "But I'm glad I did." When he leaned in, she stopped breathing.

With his lips a few inches away from hers, he trapped her in his bright green eyes. He smelled like sandalwood. The air between them heated up, and he brushed the back of his fingers over her left cheek. She shivered and breathed in. "I kissed you?" she whispered, jaggedly pushing the words past her throat.

Eight

The trailer door banged against the wall as it flew open, and Chrisna jumped back.

"Because he's a hard ass," Bran said loudly as he stomped into the trailer.

Jax followed him. "You're just overly sensitive, man."

They flopped down on the couch opposite Tyce and Chrisna, and Bran smiled at the two of them, now sitting three feet away from each other. "I told you she wouldn't put out," Bran said, and Jax punched him on his arm. "What?"

"Be nice," Jax said and looked at Chrisna. "Ignore him, Kristen, he's an ass."

"It's Kris*tal*," Tyce corrected him.

"Wait a second." Bran shifted forward on the couch and placed his elbows on his knees. "Kristal?" He looked at Tyce. "She's the girl you were going on—"

"Where's Zenelda?" Tyce asked.

"She's still with the other guys. Bran here tried to kick Asher's ass because he couldn't beat him at arm wrestling. Like he could take him in a fight. So I had to drag him out of there."

Bran folded his arms and leaned back against the couch. "He cheated, and I could've beaten him."

"Yeah, yeah. You couldn't beat an egg."

Chrisna put the beer bottle on the floor, picked up her purse and stood up. "I better go." She glanced at her watch, 12.45am.

Tyce jumped up. "I'll walk you out."

"There's a bed right there!" Bran yelled as they stepped out of the trailer, and Chrisna heard him scream, "Ouch!" just before Tyce closed the door behind them.

When Chrisna stepped onto the ground, Tyce grabbed her hand and pulled her into the shade behind the trailer. "I'm sorry," he said, looking at her. "This wasn't how I wanted it to go."

"You had a plan?" She smiled nervously and pushed her glasses up on the bridge of her nose.

"Yes, well…" He grinned and rubbed the back of his neck, "not exactly. I was surprised when I saw you to-night. After our conversation at the café, I honestly didn't think…" He looked down at her hand that he was still holding and pushed his fingers in between hers. "But then I saw you in front of the stage…"

A tingling feeling shot up her fingers, through her arm and down her spine. "Was that song about me?" she whispered and looked down at his other hand cupping hers.

"A little," he said.

She looked up at him. "A little?" she asked. "Like 'sometimes'?"

He smiled his smile and she couldn't move. If she didn't say something, she knew she was going to kiss him. So she said the first thing that came to mind. "Did I really kiss you?"

Still smiling, Tyce closed the small gap between them, leaned in, and just before his lips touched hers, she yawned.

Quickly pulling out of his grip, she pushed her hand in front of her mouth. "Skees," she said, her cheeks burning.

He grinned. "Am I boring you?"

"No, of course not. It's just that it's been a long—"

"I'm joking," he said. "I'm not good at making jokes but sometimes I get a laugh, or at least a chuckle." He looked down at his hand and rubbed a thin line of blood from a fresh scrape on his finger. "You're still wearing your wedding ring I see."

Chrisna glanced at her ring, and then at his hand where the setting must've cut him when she pulled away. "I'm sorry," she said.

"For cutting my hand?" Tyce grinned. "Or for still wearing your ring?"

Chrisna frowned, offended that he'd think that she should apologize for still wearing her ring. It had nothing to do with him.

"Okay. That was a bad joke."

"Kristal!" She heard Zenelda calling.

"I have to go," she said.

"You're angry."

She sighed deeply. "No, I'm not," she lied. "But I really do have to go."

"There you guys are," Zenelda said when she appeared around the corner of the trailer. "Come on, we're playing '*Gargle a Song*', and I'm kicking ass and taking names."

"It's okay," Tyce said, "I think the guys want to go back to the hotel."

Zenelda frowned. "Don't be silly, now come on."

Tyce glanced at Chrisna, who quickly looked at the ground.

"Freeze the fire," Zenelda said. "What's going on here?"

Chrisna looked up. "Nothing, let's go." She pulled the strap of her purse higher up on her shoulder and walked past Zenelda.

"Stop!" Zenelda yelled, and Chrisna stopped in her tracks. "What's the matter?"

She turned back. "I said it's nothing."

Zenelda turned to Tyce. "Why is she upset?"

"I said something stupid."

"You told her?" Zenelda asked. "Are you crazy?"

Chrisna walked back to where they stood. "Told me what?"

"No. I didn't," Tyce said.

"Told me what?" Chrisna repeated.

Zenelda didn't answer, and Tyce looked very uncomfortable.

"Tyce?" Chrisna asked.

"It was a long time ago, I—"

"Don't freak out," Zenelda said and stepped in front of Chrisna, taking her by the shoulders. "We... had a thing."

Chrisna's jaw dropped. "You mean you slept together?" she inquired as she stepped back out of Zenelda's hold.

"It was almost ten years ago," Zenelda said. "And it only happened once. Don't be angry."

Chrisna waited a few seconds before she was able to speak. "I'm not angry that you slept together ten years ago. I only just met both of you." She looked past Zenelda at Tyce. "But why didn't you tell me when I asked you about her earlier?"

Tyce didn't have time to answer before Zenelda spoke again, "Don't be angry with him."

Chrisna looked at her. "Weren't you already married ten years ago?"

"Yes," Zenelda almost whispered, looking embarrassed.

Chrisna felt her throat tighten and her thoughts glazed over. She *was* angry, but she wasn't sure exactly why. Was it because Tyce wasn't honest with her when she asked him why he was so uncomfortable around Zenelda? Was it because Zenelda didn't tell her when she asked her how she knew Tyce? Or was it because Tyce commented on her still wearing her ring? She couldn't figure out what exactly it was that caused her to feel so upset. "I have to go," she said and turned around, hurrying away.

"Kristal!" Zenelda called after her.

"My name's *not* Kristal!" Chrisna shouted and quickened her steps.

As she passed a few of the other trailers, Chrisna realized that the music had stopped and crewmembers were packing up the area for the night. Not really knowing in which direction to go and feeling suddenly exhausted, she walked past the last trailer and sat down against a rusty lamppost, with a blown bulb, near another chain-linked fence.

It was quiet except for the continuous drone of the people passing by on the other side of the fence. She placed her purse down next to her and pulled her knees against her chest, thankful for the small patch of darkness surrounding her.

She couldn't be angry with Zenelda. How was she supposed to slip that piece of information into the time it took for them to walk from the second guard to the trailer? She couldn't be angry with Tyce. Who tells someone something like that during their second conversation, or third, if you counted the night she couldn't remember? Besides, he didn't know that she knew Zenelda before tonight. Lifting her left hand, she stared at her wedding ring. She was angry with herself. Frustrated, tired, and embarrassed about storming off. She wiped the tears with the back of her hand before they could escape.

There are only three reasons one should ever cry:

When you're listening to great music – There was no

music playing.

When you're truly happy – She was far from being happy.

When somebody needs you to cry – No one needed her.

She heard static noise coming from her purse, and when she opened it, she listened to a voice distorting over the butterfly walkie-talkie pushed in between her notepad and cell phone in one of the compartments. She must've forgotten to switch it off earlier. Lifting it out of her bag, she heard Zenelda's voice. "You there?"

Chrisna looked at the device.

"If you can hear me, please answer," Zenelda said, and the speaker emitted static again. "Sexy. Opus. Radio. Radio. Yellow."

Chrisna thought about the words for a second and then realized that Zenelda was trying to spell '*sorry*' by using her own twisted version of the Military Phonetic Alphabet.

Zenelda's wacky attempt made her smile and she felt a little better. She pressed the yellow butterfly on the walkie-talkie. "Sierra. Oscar. Romeo. Romeo. Yankee," she said, recalling what she'd learned in the *Voortrekker Youth Organization* when she was in primary school. She released the button.

"Are you okay?" Zenelda asked.

Chrisna pressed the button again. "I overreacted."

"That's okay. It's under-reacting that pisses me off."

Chrisna smiled again. "Is Tyce listening?"

"No. Walkie-talkies are for secrets, remember?"

Chrisna breathed in and then slowly exhaled. "Then tell me one."

There was a long pause before Zenelda said, "I can't whistle."

Chrisna chuckled. "That's not a secret, it's a disability."

"Can *you* whistle?"

Lifting her left hand, Chrisna pressed her thumb and middle finger together, moistened her lips and pulled them back over her teeth, placed her fingers underneath the tip of her tongue, tightly closed her lips over them, and blew as hard as she could. A piercing '*phewww*' sound cut through the air.

"Nuclear Boom!" Zenelda said a few seconds later. "I heard that without the walkie-talkie."

Chrisna then realized that she'd forgotten to push the button. She pressed the butterfly again. "Now tell me a *real* secret."

A few seconds of silence followed before Zenelda spoke again. "My husband never knew that I had cheated on him."

"Why did you?"

"The life I lead before I got married wasn't exactly a conventional one."

Chrisna thought about her own life and how it was nothing but conventional.

Zenelda continued, "I guess sleeping with Tyce was my way of trying to get back what I once had, but as soon as it happened I knew it wasn't what I wanted anymore. It wasn't who I was anymore, and I accepted that I'd changed. Telling Joe would've only hurt him."

"Don't you think you owed it to him to be honest?"

"Tyce once said those exact words to me," Zenelda said. "About four years ago, after he'd played a set at my store, he said that he wanted to tell Joe what we did, that he needed to own up to his mistakes, make it right, but I wouldn't let him. It turned into a huge fight and he left. That was the last time I saw him before tonight."

Chrisna didn't know how to respond and a long pause followed before Zenelda spoke again. "Tyce is a good guy. Sure, he used to have a wild streak but he changed."

Chrisna breathed in. "Changed how?"

"Let me put it this way, if some families are filthy rich, his was soiled, and I'm not just talking about money. He grew up as a very spoiled only-child and his father openly cheated on his mother, but she stayed with him regardless. I think that hurt him a lot. When his father wanted him to give up his music and go into the family business, he rebelled and was cut off and thrown out of the house. His life got a lot crazier after that. His music seemed to be the only thing that grounded him at times. It was only about five years ago, when his father passed away, that he reunited with his mother. Since then, he's done really well for himself. His father had left him a lot of money in his will and Tyce used it to start a free afterschool music program for inner-city kids across London."

The only word Chrisna could utter was, "Wow."

"Now *you* tell *me* a secret."

Chrisna breathed in again before pressing the yellow butterfly. "I think I like him."

"Tyce? That's not a secret, sweetie."

Chrisna heard Zenelda giggle before she heard static again. "It's not?"

"No."

"Oh."

"He likes you too."

A tingle ran down Chrisna's spine. "He does?"

"I know Tyce, and I saw the way he looked at you. He never used to look at normal girls like that."

Chrisna thought about the words '*normal girls*'. Normal? It probably was the best way to describe her life, well at least up to the point she got divorced. No, even after that. She was normal and she didn't like it. "I don't want to be *normal* anymore," she said.

"I didn't mean it like that."

"Tell me who she is."

"Who?"

"Kristal. Is she another character from a book?"

"No. She's *you*," Zenelda said. "Well, the '*you*' I thought I saw when we first met. I didn't really buy into the introverted, scared, reserved person you were pretending to be."

"I wasn't pretending."

"You sure?"

Chrisna didn't answer and Zenelda continued. "Anyway, the name Kristal popped into my head."

"But what's she like?"

"You tell me," Zenelda said.

Chrisna looked at her wedding ring again. It bothered her that she still wasn't ready to get rid of it and she wasn't sure why. But maybe if she could open herself up to what life was throwing at her and just enjoy the intrigue, maybe then she could find the person she wanted to be, and then maybe she could let go. And if being *Kristal* was a way to do it, then maybe she should try to be her, whoever she was.

"Are you still there, Chrisna?" Zenelda asked.

"It's Kilo. Romeo. India. Sierra. Tango. Alpha. Lima."

There was a brief pause before Zenelda replied. "Baby. Opus. Opus. Mama."

Chrisna laughed before pressing the button again. "Could you give the walkie-talkie to Tyce, please?"

"Sure, hold on. Out."

Chrisna waited nervously, not sure if Tyce would want to talk to her. She placed the walkie-talkie on the ground next to her, pulled her cell phone out of her purse, unlocked it, and pressed the gallery button. Flipping through the photos of the party, she stopped and looked at the close up one of Tyce pulling a face. She smiled and then dragged her finger across the screen a few more times. When she passed the photo of her leaning over the rail, just before she apparently tossed her glasses overboard, she saw that there were pictures she hadn't seen before. She saw one where she was dancing with Tyce, one of the guests must've taken it. Her arms were wrapped around his neck, and he was holding her around her waist. She felt her cheeks heat up again.

Dragging her finger over the screen, she scrolled to the next picture. They were holding each other in the same way as they had in the previous photo but this time her arms were tightly wrapped around his neck. She scrolled again, and then she gasped. Her lips were pressed against his.

Gaping at the photo for a few more seconds, she closed the App. and opened her internet browser, typing his name into the search engine. She read the list that appeared on the screen, but one news heading stood out. '*Music Patron Honored for Humanitarianism*'. Staring at the article, she read, '*Tyce Turcotte, better known as the lead guitarist of Solid Flint, has been recognized for services to the community and the arts, for his contribution...*'

She heard his voice. "Hi, Kristal." Her throat tightened and she held her breath for a second.

Locking her phone, she returned it to her purse, and picked up the walkie-talkie. "Hi," she said softly. "I'm sorry I stormed off."

"I'm sorry I didn't tell you. You have every right to be angry."

"No, I don't. I'm sorry."

"Me too."

She smiled. "Do you think those were enough apologies?"

"I guess." She heard the amusement in his voice.

"Oh, wait, one more. I'm sorry that I kissed you." She teased.

"You are?"

"I found the photo on my phone just now and it looks like I bulldozed you." She grinned.

"Look closely and you'll see that I'm not putting up much of a fight." There was a slight pause before he spoke again. "Zenelda said that you wanted to tell me a secret."

Her stomach turned. "She did?"

"Yes."

A lump stuck in her throat and she breathed in quickly. "I can whistle."

"Zenelda told me that it was you earlier, waking up the neighborhood." Tyce laughed his warm laugh. "Very impressive."

"You heard our conversation?" She asked anxiously, hoping that Zenelda hadn't been lying when she'd said Tyce couldn't hear them.

"No, I was in the trailer. When I heard the whistle, I stepped out and Zenelda said that it was you."

She sighed with relief.

"So, what was the secret you wanted to tell me?" he asked.

Chrisna glanced at her ring. She wanted to be honest with him, but how was she supposed to tell him why she was still wearing her wedding ring when she wasn't sure herself. She liked him but she didn't want to lead him on, that wouldn't be fair to either one of them. Taking a deep breath, she said, "I really want us to be friends." As she said it, she regretted it.

There was a long pause before Tyce replied in an even tone, "Sure."

She tried to swallow down the lump in her throat before speaking again. "Skees, but my life is just too..." She paused, searching for the word.

"Complicated?" he asked.

"Ja," she said, although the word didn't begin to describe what she wanted to say.

"I understand. Do you want to come back to the trailer now so we can toast our new found friendship?"

She wasn't sure if he was being sarcastic but it didn't sound that way to her, he sounded more concerned than anything else. "I'll be there in a sec."

"Over and out," he said, and it made her smile.

Switching off the walkie-talkie, she placed it in her purse, stood up, and dusted off her jeans, before heading back.

She took slower, more tentative steps as she neared the trailer but when she saw Tyce waiting for her outside, a huge smile spread over her face. He smiled when he saw her.

"Did you call off the search party?" She teased.

"I was just about to," he said and stepped forward, wrapping his arms around her and hugging her tightly.

He'd caught her off guard. Her one arm pressed against his chest and she lifted the other as far up his back as she could reach. She felt his warm breath on her neck and inhaled his sandalwood scent. Her heart dropped to her stomach as she, once again, regretted her decision to *just* be his friend.

When he let go, she exhaled slowly.

"Come on, Zenelda's inside," he said and opened the trailer door for her.

"And your friends?" she asked, not looking forward to seeing Bran again.

"They went back to the hotel."

As she stepped inside, Zenelda jumped up from the couch and almost pushed her over as she threw her arms around her neck and squeezed. Chrisna couldn't remember ever being hugged that tightly in her life, but it didn't compare to the closeness she'd felt when Tyce had just hugged her.

"Okay, glad to see you, too." Chrisna groaned. "You can let go now, I won't leave again."

Zenelda stepped back. "Promise?"

She looked more serious than she'd ever seen her and Chrisna frowned. "Okay, I promise. I won't leave again."

Sitting down on the couch standing on the right, Zenelda picked up a beer off the floor and took a long sip.

Tyce handed Chrisna a full bottle and they both sat down on the other couch, but this time, Tyce left a large space between them.

Placing her purse on the floor, Chrisna took a sip of her beer, but Tyce held his up in the air. "To friendship," he said, and Zenelda frowned.

"Wait," Chrisna said, and Tyce pulled the bottle away from his mouth. She looked from him to Zenelda. "Have you two sorted things out?"

"What do you mean?" he frowned.

"She told me about the fight you had," Chrisna said, "the last time you saw each other."

Zenelda cleared her throat. "It's okay. We're good. Right, Tyce?"

He lowered his bottle and cupped it with both hands, looking down. "Actually, there's something I need to tell you." He looked up at Zenelda. "After I left the store that night, I went to your house."

Zenelda gaped at him. "What did you do?"

He cleared his throat. "I told Joe what happened between us."

"You did *what*?" Zenelda raised her voice.

"I had to. I'm sorry I went behind your back."

Zenelda stared at him.

"I'm really sorry," Tyce said.

"So he knew," Zenelda almost whispered. "He never said anything." She leaned back on the couch and stared up at the ceiling.

Chrisna shifted closer to Tyce, touched his knee, and whispered in his ear, "You did the right thing."

Placing his hand over hers, he looked at her and forced a grin. "But I handled it badly," he said and pulled his hand away. Looking at Zenelda, he shifted a few inches away from Chrisna.

Chrisna pulled her hand back and watched him for a few seconds before looking at Zenelda, still staring at the ceiling. "Are you okay?" Chrisna asked.

Zenelda lifted her hand in a stop-motion without looking at her, and she held it there for a moment before lowering it, sitting up, and then looking at Tyce. "I forgive you," she said. "Now how about a song?"

Chrisna frowned. "Are you sure you're—"

"She's fine," Tyce said, sounding curt, and then he looked at Chrisna and smiled. "We're fine," he said, softer this time, and she wasn't sure if he was referring to him and Zenelda, or to him and her.

"Amaze me," Zenelda said, standing in front of Tyce with his acoustic guitar in hand.

He took the guitar from her and shifted even farther away from Chrisna, placing his beer on the floor and positioning the guitar on his lap. "What do you want to hear?"

Sitting down again, Zenelda stretched her arms over the back of the couch and said, "One of yours, of course."

He strummed the strings and then stopped the sound with his palm, thinking for a moment.

"Remember that song you wrote about the sidewalk?" Zenelda asked.

Tyce grinned. "That's silly."

"It's always been one of my favorites," Zenelda said. "Come on, give it a go."

"Okay." He took a deep breath and then picked the

strings. "*There are small steps I take with the progress I make, as I'm walking through the rain. And I stop and I stare at the people that wear, their masks all day in vain. But I look at my feet, avoiding the street, I'm on the same path again. Where there are cracks on the sidewalk, cracks in the air, even cracks in this refrain.*" He stopped for a second and then flicked his fingers over the strings as fast as he could.

Zenelda burst out laughing. Tyce stopped and laughed with her. Chrisna grinned as she looked at the two of them, and she knew they were okay.

"Can we try something you both know now?" Tyce asked, tucking his hair in behind his ear. "So you can sing along?"

Zenelda used her beer to point to Chrisna. "*She* only sings in elevators."

Chrisna pushed her glasses up on the bridge of her nose as Tyce looked at her. "Long story," she said.

"They got stuck," Zenelda said. "He sang, she sang, they sang."

Chrisna grinned. "Okay, maybe not that long."

"Do Blades of Blue," Zenelda said and winked at her. "She loves them."

Tyce grinned and glanced at her. "Then you'll know this one," he said and strummed the strings again.

Chrisna smiled as she listened to him singing '*Dying Twice*'. Zenelda started singing along but just before they reached the chorus, Tyce stopped and frowned at Chrisna. "Come on."

She smiled shyly and shook her head as she took a long sip of her beer.

Tyce and Zenelda belted out the chorus and then Zenelda stopped, leaving Tyce to sing solo. When he hit the chorus again, she fell in, and Chrisna couldn't stop herself from singing along. Halfway through it, both Zenelda and Tyce almost stopped simultaneously to let Chrisna sing the rest of the chorus, watching her as she sang.

Feeling uncomfortable, she stopped when the chorus ended. "Why did you stop?"

Zenelda gaped at her. "I didn't know you could sing like that."

Blushing, Chrisna shifted back on the couch.

"I like your voice, it's a sultry kind of husky," Tyce said and turned to Zenelda. "Doesn't her voice remind you of—?"

"Play something else." Chrisna interrupted him, trying to conceal her embarrassment.

Zenelda grinned.

"Please," Chrisna said. "But this time I'm just listening."

"Well, since you like Blades of Blue, this is one of my favorites." He picked the strings and played a slow melody.

Chrisna's body numbed when she recognized the song. It was '*Scattered Tears*', the song she'd listened to over and over again after her divorce. When he started singing, she felt herself tearing up, so she placed her beer on the floor, leaned back into the couch again, and closed her eyes. She tried to control her breathing as she concentrated on his voice and not the words.

Nine

Chrisna knew she wasn't in her hotel room as she felt the warm leather push against her left arm. She slowly opened her eyes and saw a blurred image of Zenelda, sleeping on the black leather couch opposite her.

In trying to move, she felt something holding her down, and when she looked, she saw an arm stretching over her chest and a hand holding onto hers. Carefully turning her head, she saw Tyce's face on the armrest behind her. He was positioned against the back of the couch, spooning her. She turned her head back when Zenelda stirred.

Breathing in slowly and then exhaling quietly, she was surprised to find that she felt comfortable in Tyce's arms for some reason, relaxed and safe and that unsettled her. She took another breath and carefully slipped her hand out of his, lifting his arm.

He sighed and she froze.

After a couple of seconds, she moved his arm again and gently placed it behind her back. He stirred and she held her breath.

"Good morning." Tyce mumbled sleepily and she

turned cold.

When she felt him turning his body farther onto his side, as if trying to move away from her, she whispered, "Good morning," and turned onto her back, looking at him.

Tyce propped himself up on one elbow and looked down at her. "Did you sleep well?" he asked softly.

"I did," she whispered, not lying.

"Good," he said and tried to push himself up even more, but his hand slipped off the armrest and he dropped, stopping his face an inch from hers.

His chest pressed against hers and she wasn't sure whose heart was beating so rapidly against her ribs, but she knew hers was hastily pumping the warmth through her body.

She wanted him to kiss her, but he merely smiled, breathed in deeply and pushed himself up and away from her.

Closing her eyes for a second, she sighed, rolled her body off the couch and stood up. Retying her ponytail, she whispered, "My glasses?"

He stretched over the armrest and reached down beside the couch, lifting her glasses off the floor and handing them to her.

Quickly pushing them onto her nose, she saw Tyce throwing his legs over the edge of the cushions, placing his feet on the floor, lifting his arms in the air, and stretching his back.

She caught a glimpse of his toned stomach muscles

when his shirt lifted a few inches, and felt a sensation she had not felt in years stirring in her abdomen.

Tyce smiled and she looked down, only then realizing that her camisole had rolled up to just above her bellybutton. Quickly pulling on the hem, she stretched it as far down as it would go without exposing her breasts. She blushed and glanced at her watch, 6.17am. Her eyes caught a glimpse of a backstage pass lying on the floor next to the couch, and she only then realized that she wasn't wearing hers anymore. Someone must've removed it while she was asleep. Picking it up, she asked, "Do I still need this?"

Tyce wiped the sleep from his eyes. "No, you're with me," he said, and for a moment she liked the way that sounded.

She looked at Zenelda and then saw that her pass was also on the floor next to the couch she was sleeping on. Picking it up, she asked, "Can I keep them?"

Tyce frowned. "Sure."

Chrisna placed both passes in her purse and looked at Zenelda, who stirred again.

"Do you think we should wake her?" Tyce asked.

Stretched out across the couch, Zenelda breathed loudly. "I don't know," Chrisna whispered and turned back to face him. "You know her better than I do. Will she kill us if we wake her up?"

He grinned. "If I remember correctly, she might."

"So what do we do?"

Tyce stood up. "Let's get some coffee," he said. "She

might kill us a little less if we bring her coffee."

Chrisna smiled.

After she'd used the small restroom in the back of the trailer where the bed stood, Chrisna waited for Tyce to freshen up before they tiptoed out the door.

It was already light out and the area around the trailers was quiet, but when they exited through the gate near the chain-linked fence, she saw a horde of people streaming into the side streets where the stands had been the night before.

"Wait," she said and stopped. "I forgot my purse."

He smiled. "Don't worry, it's my treat."

When they walked past the fountain with the green and black mermaids, Tyce stopped. "You fancy a bath?" He grinned.

"I wouldn't mind bathing, but not right now, thanks."

He narrowed his eyes and then swept her off her feet, carrying her to the fountain.

She shrieked. "What are you doing?"

He stopped, pressed his knees against the edge of the fountain and leaned forward, holding her above the water. "You sure you don't want to bath? Friends tell friends when they stink."

Chrisna would've slapped him, had it not been for the fact that both her hands were holding onto his neck for dear life. He feigned losing his grip on her for a split second, dropping her a few inches, and she shrieked again. "Tyce, no!"

He quickly lifted her higher and when he put her down, his expression pained. Tyce wiggled his index finger in his ear. "You sure can hit a note!" he exclaimed, grinning.

"That was cruel," she said, folding her arms. "How would you like it if I did that to you?"

He smiled. "You can try."

Glaring at him for a second, she leaned down, put her hand in the water, and splashed him.

He flinched. "You did *not* just do that," he said, wiping his face with his shirt.

"Now we're even."

"Not even close," he said and reached for the water.

Chrisna backed away and ran around him in the direction of the obelisk.

"You're not going to make me catch you, are you?" She heard Tyce yell and she looked behind her.

He wasn't even trying to catch up to her, so she stopped and waited.

When he neared her, he sprinted forward and picked her up again, throwing her over his shoulder.

"Put me down!" she yelled and hit him on his back.

"You know, hitting me is not going to help you," he said, amused, and continued carrying her as he casually walked on. "There's another fountain up ahead. You might consider apologizing right about now."

She stopped hitting him and glanced at the passersby who stared at them. "Okay, I'm sorry, but you started it."

"Real apologies don't have a '*but*' in them," he said.

"Okay, fine. I. Am. Sorry."

He stopped and let her down. "That wasn't so difficult, was it?"

Placing her hands on her hips, she glared at him again. "Don't you need a license to be this mean?"

Folding his arms, he frowned. "You think I'm mean?"

"I might not," she said and grinned, "if you take a swim in *that* fountain." She pointed to the second fountain behind him.

"Is that a dare?"

She folded her arms and copied his stance. "Ja."

Tyce grinned, unfolded his arms, took his wallet and cell phone out of his pockets, and handed them to Chrisna. "Okay then."

She gaped at him. "You're actually going to do it?"

"Well, I don't want you to think I'm mean," he said, walking toward the fountain.

"I wasn't serious, you know."

He glanced back at her. "Then you shouldn't have dared me."

Hurrying after him, she stopped a few feet away as he stopped beside the fountain, lifting his one leg and looking at her again.

"Fine," she said and folded her arms again, watching him. "Go ahead."

He lifted his foot over the edge and stepped forward, leaving his other leg to dangle over the edge. The water pushed over his hip.

"Okay, you made your point," she said. "We can go now."

Pulling his other leg over, he slowly lowered it into the water. "It's freezing," he said and pretended to shiver. "I might get pneumonia but as long as you don't think I'm mean."

"You're insane," she said and stepped forward, stopping next to the fountain.

He grinned. "You did say '*swim*', right?"

She shook her head. "No."

He smiled. "Yes, you did." Lifting his arms above his shoulders, he fell backward, and the water splashed over the edge.

Chrisna stepped back, avoiding the splatter, and then leaned forward and saw Tyce splashing through the water as he attempted the backstroke.

"Jou kop raas," she said.

He stopped and frowned at her. "What does *that* mean?"

She smiled. "Ask Zenelda."

Turning onto his stomach, he stood up, pushed the hair out of his face, walked toward her, and held out his hand. "Help me out?" he asked. His soaked t-shirt stuck to his body, accentuating every muscle.

Stepping back, she shook her head. "Not a chance."

"Come on. I might be mean but I'm not cruel."

Frowning, she stepped forward again, placed his cell phone and wallet on the edge of the fountain, and took his hand. "Okay. I trust you."

Grinning, he held out his other hand, and taking it, she pulled him forward. He lifted his one leg over the edge but before he could shift his weight, she let go of his hand and pushed him backward.

"Who's the mean one now?" he asked when he lifted his head out of the water and stood up again.

"That would be *me*," she said, and then she wondered what *Kristal* would do at that moment. She removed her glasses, placing them on the edge near his wallet and phone, and then she grinned. Pushing herself up on the edge, she threw her legs over and lunged forward, taking him down with her as she plunged into the cold water.

"*You're* insane," he said when he lifted his head out of the water. Quickly standing up again, he held out his hand to her.

She struggled to get her footing as she reached for his hand, but his grip was strong and he easily pulled her out of the water.

Wiping a few wet strands of hair out of her face, she said, "I didn't think I could do that."

"You are full of surprises," he said, pushing his hair out of his face again.

"You were right." She shivered. "The water *is* freezing."

"Come on," he said and walked to the edge of the fountain. He put his hands around her waist and she shivered again, but not from the cold. Quickly lifting her, he helped her up and over the edge, gently putting her down on the other side.

"Thanks," she grinned, and he leaped over and onto the ground.

Her whole body shook when she pushed her glasses back onto her nose.

"We better get you back and into some dry clothes," he said, picking up his wallet and cell phone.

She rubbed her upper arms, trying to get warm. "No, let's get that coffee."

"Are you sure? I don't want you to catch a cold."

"I'm sure," she said and shivered again.

They hurried into Rue Royale, and Chrisna glanced at the people putting their goods out on the stands.

Stopping in front of a café with red awnings above the arched windows, Tyce leaned against the glass door and peered in. "What time is it?" he asked and turned to her.

Looking at her watch, she said, "Six thirty-five."

Tyce sighed. "I think we're a little early."

She shivered again and folded her arms over her chest, tightly gripping her upper arms.

"You're cold," he said, stepped toward her, pushed his cell phone and wallet under his arm, and rubbed her upper arms with both hands. "Your lips are blue," he whispered.

"I'm fine," she lied, her voice shaking.

He lifted his head, looked past her and then took her hand, pulling her farther down the street. She hurried to keep up with him and then she saw the small stand with the word '*Café*' written on a large sign above it.

"Trois cafés, s'il vous plait," Tyce said when they stopped in front of the stand.

Chrisna tried to control her breathing as her body continued to shake, and a couple of minutes later, the pasty man placed three paper cups on the counter.

Tyce took some money from his wallet and paid the man before handing Chrisna one of the cups. She eagerly took a sip, scorching her tongue.

"Careful, it's hot," Tyce said, placing his wallet and cell phone under his arm again and lifting the other two cups. "Don't you want some sugar?" he asked.

She shook her head as she blew on the steam.

"Would you mind putting five sugars into this one?" He held up one of the cups.

Chrisna's eyebrows shot up, her mouth pulling into a comical, skew grimace.

"It's Zenelda's," he said and forced a grin.

Pouring the sugar into the cup, Chrisna stirred it, and then covered both cups with lids before pushing one over the rim of her cup.

"Thanks," Tyce said, smiling before they hurried back to the trailer.

A light breeze blew against Chrisna's wet clothes and she shivered again, taking another sip of her coffee.

By the time they'd reached the trailer, her cup was empty and she hurried past Tyce to open the trailer door for him.

"Thanks," he said and stepped in.

Zenelda jumped to her feet when Chrisna closed the door too loudly.

"Skees," Chrisna said, stepping into the trailer and placing her empty cup on the table.

Zenelda stared at them with wide eyes, still looking half asleep. "What the hell? What time is it?" she asked and flopped back down on the couch.

Chrisna looked at her watch. "Six thirty-five," she said and frowned. Holding her wrist up to her ear and then looking at it again, she shook it before looking at Tyce. "I think we drowned my watch."

He grinned. "We?"

She grinned. "I."

"Is that for me?" Zenelda asked and rubbed her eyes.

"Oh, yes, sorry." Tyce handed her the cup.

Taking a sip, she looked at him. "How many sugars did you put in this?"

"Five," Chrisna answered.

Zenelda grinned. "Just checking, thanks." She took another sip and looked at the two of them in their soaked clothes. "What happened?'

"We didn't want to use the shower in here because we were afraid we'd wake you." Tyce grinned, winking at Chrisna. "So we went for a swim."

"Well, as long as you had fun," Zenelda said, not sounding fully awake yet.

Chrisna looked at Tyce and forced a grin as her whole body shook.

"Speaking of which," he said, placing his cup, cell phone, and wallet on the table next to the fridge, and taking Chrisna's hand, pulling her toward the back of the trailer.

"What are you doing?" she asked, her voice shaking.

"You'll thank me in a minute," he said.

When they entered the room, he left her standing beside the bed as he walked into the small restroom, opening the shower faucets.

Chrisna stood frozen, her lips quivered and she struggled to breath normally.

"The water will warm you up," he said and pushed his hand under the steaming spray.

Chrisna's teeth clattered as she tried to speak. "I...can't...move."

Tyce turned around, walked toward her, carefully lifted her glasses off her face, placed them on the bed, and lifted her off her feet.

Stepping into the small cubicle, he slowly set her down as the hot water sprayed onto both of them, and Chrisna gasped when the warmth scalded her skin.

"Is it too hot?" he asked and reached for the hot water faucet.

She grabbed his hand and pulled it back. "No."

The water streamed down both their faces as Tyce looked down at her, pushing a strand of hair out of her eyes.

A sudden heat surged through her and she wasn't sure that it was entirely the water's doing. She leaned forward into his chest, and he wrapped his arms around her. She could feel him breathing in and out slowly and, matching her breathing to his, her body gradually stopped shaking.

"Thank you." She sighed, a minute or so later, and looked up.

The water streamed down Tyce's face and onto hers. "You're welcome," he said softly, and then let go of her before stepping out of the shower and closing the door behind him.

She watched his blurred image moving behind the tempered glass.

"You should get rid of those clothes," he said loudly.

She looked down at her soaking wet camisole, jeans, and ballet pumps. "I don't have anything else to wear."

Tyce didn't reply, and with a lot of effort, she pulled her camisole over her head, took off her shoes, jeans, and underwear, and placed them in a bundle on the floor, in one of the corners. She looked at her broken watch, untied the strap and pushed it into her jeans pocket.

Looking around, she found a combination men's shampoo and shower gel, untied her hair, placing the band on the empty soap dish. After she had washed her hair and body, she rinsed her clothes. When she was done, she sighed, not wanting to get out. But she closed the faucets and opened the door a fraction, peering out.

The door leading to the adjacent room was closed and she saw a thick bath towel on the closed toilet seat. Stepping out, she reached for the towel and dried her body and her hair as best she could. The long, dark brown strands fell onto her shoulders and she wrapped the towel around her body, hung her wet clothes over the towel rail, and placed her shoes underneath it, before opening the door.

Tyce sat on the bed. He'd changed into a pair of blue jeans, blue trainers, and a black t-shirt with a blue paint-splatter pattern on it. When she stepped out, his jaw dropped a little as he gaped at her.

Even though her body was still warm from the shower, she could feel her cheeks heat up as she felt a little exposed with just the towel around her.

Tyce cleared his throat as he averted his eyes, tucking his damp hair in behind his ear. Then he stood up, and handed her glasses to her. "Feeling better?" he asked.

Pushing her glasses onto her nose, she said, "Much better, thank you."

Tyce stared at her for a moment longer before turning toward the bed and lifting a set of clothes off the covers, handing them to her. "I'm not sure if they'll fit but it's all I have. There is a drawstring."

She squinted at the men's sweatpants and black t-shirt. "It will have to do I guess," she said and smiled before returning to the bathroom to put on the clothes. She had to roll the waistband down around her hips a couple of times and the t-shirt was about two sizes too big but it covered a lot more skin than a towel.

When she stepped out again, she frowned.

"What's wrong?" he asked.

Glancing down, she wiggled her toes. "My shoes are wet."

"Oh, right," Tyce said. "I might have something that could work." He hurried around the bed and picked up a black backpack off the floor, opened it, and poured the contents out onto the covers. At least ten pairs of flip-flops in various sizes fell onto the bed. "We bought these from a charity foundation the other day. For every pair you buy, they donate one pair of school shoes to under-privileged children in Africa." He picked up a pink pair, walked over to her, placed them on the floor in front of her feet, and stepped back. "Bran thought it would be a good idea to buy various sizes for his lady-friends if they stayed over."

"Do *you* have any '*lady-friends*' that stay over?" she teased, quizzically peering at him from underneath the veil of her dark locks. She instantly felt ashamed about prying into such personal affairs the moment the words left her mouth. She looked down and pushed her feet into the flip-flops, trying to think of something smarter to say, or perhaps a way to smooth over that silly question.

"A couple," Tyce deadpanned before she could open her mouth to say anything else.

Chrisna gaped at him, surprised that he would share such detail with her. "You do?"

He grinned coyly. "Yes. You and Zenelda."

Smiling, Chrisna looked back down at her feet. "They fit, thank you," she said.

"Can I come in yet?!" Zenelda yelled. "I have to use the toilet."

Chrisna blushed. "Come in."

A second later, Zenelda burst through the door and raced to the toilet, slamming the door shut behind her.

Tyce grinned, shaking his head, and Chrisna followed him out of the room.

She sat down on the couch on the left and he sat down on the couch opposite her.

"So," he said. "Do you have any big plans for today?"

Chrisna thought about all the things she had scheduled on her itinerary, and then she glanced at her wrist where her watch used to be. Rubbing the skin, she looked up at Tyce. *Kristal* wouldn't go back to sightseeing alone after all that's happened, would she? "No," she said aloud.

"Yes, she does," Zenelda said, standing in the doorway. "We're going shopping."

Ten

Chrisna followed Zenelda over the Pont de la Concorde Bridge as they crossed the Seine, Chrisna gripping her purse in front of her chest as she glanced at the riverboats on either side of the bridge.

Before they'd left the trailer, Zenelda had taken a shower, and then she commented on how she was going '*commando*' until she could buy some new clothes and underwear.

Chrisna pushed her purse tighter against her chest. She too was going '*commando*', and she felt extremely self-conscious about doing so. She'd never gone out in public without wearing a bra or panties before.

"You know, we could've just gone back to my hotel to get a change of clothes," Chrisna said.

"Where's the fun in that?" Zenelda asked. "Besides, we have to get you something stunning to wear for tonight."

"I have a nice floral summer dress I can wear."

Zenelda frowned. "A summer dress? Tyce is taking us to *The Purple Cross*. You won't get in wearing a summer dress."

Thinking about the wardrobe she'd packed for her trip, she realized that wherever Tyce was taking them, it was probably too formal for what she owned. "Okay," she said, "but nothing too expensive. I'm kind of on a tight budget."

Zenelda grinned. "You let me worry about that. But first we have to get you out of those pajamas."

Chrisna looked up at the large building with the twelve large pillars and the words '*Assemblée Nationale*' written in gold at the top, before they turned left and followed the road at an incline.

Tyce had said that he had to go fetch Bran and Jax, so they could move all their things back to the hotel before he could meet up with them again. His exact words were, "I'd like to take you to *The Purple Cross*", and he'd looked directly at Chrisna when he said it.

Rows of tall green trees stood on either side of the long street and the branches of opposite trees almost touched one another as they formed an arbor, casting a shadow over the road. Green and white busses traveled in a separate lane on the right side of the street, and Chrisna looked at the row of scooters and motorcycles parked on the left.

"You know, Tyce has a bike," Zenelda said.

"I know. He showed it to me…" Chrisna paused. "Well, he showed it to me on his phone," she said and sighed, wishing she could remember the night she'd kissed him.

"It is a beauty, a Honda CBR1100XX Blackbird."

"And it's metallic black," Chrisna said, having no idea how to add to the conversation.

Zenelda grinned. "So what's going on between the two of you? Has he kissed you yet?"

Chrisna gaped at her. "No."

"You want me to talk to him?" Zenelda solicited.

"No!" Chrisna exclaimed.

"Why not?" Zenelda asked amused.

Chrisna looked down at her pink flip-flops slapping against the sidewalk. "I told him that we should just be friends."

Zenelda stopped. "Why, the hell, would you do that?" she asked, incredulously.

Chrisna also stopped and glanced at her wedding ring. "Because I'm an idiot."

"Apparently." Zenelda teased. "But seriously, don't be too hard on yourself." She took Chrisna's hand, touching the setting of her ring with her thumb. "It's just a ring, sweetie." She pushed her index finger against Chrisna's forehead. "Your problem lies here." She lowered her hand and pressed her finger against Chrisna's chest, over her heart. "You can't go wrong if you listen to this."

Chrisna sighed.

They continued down the street for a few more minutes, before turning slightly left into a side street, then left again at a greengrocer, where they passed the cars parked on either side of the narrow street. When they reached the end, Zenelda turned left onto a wide street, Rue de Rennes, and stopped.

"I'm starving," Zenelda said.

"I could eat," Chrisna said and smiled as her stomach rumbled at the smell of fresh baked goods coming from the bakery. She looked up at the sign reading, '*Boulangerie*' before she followed Zenelda inside.

Chrisna looked around the shop and recognized the croissants. An assortment of plain, chocolate, and some with almond shavings on them, but she stared at the leaf-shaped breads, small pastries with chocolate inside, and the rolled up dough with the raisins on them.

"What would you like?" Zenelda asked.

With too much to choose from, Chrisna looked at Zenelda and asked, "What are you having?"

"Two of the Pain au Chocolat, but they're very sweet. I don't think you'll like them."

"I'll just have a croissant," Chrisna said, trying to pronounce the word as French as possible.

Zenelda smiled and turned to the woman behind the glass counter. "One croissant with Parma Ham and Edam cheese and two Pain au Chocolat, s'il vous plait."

"I don't like cheese," Chrisna almost whispered.

Zenelda gaped at her and mouthed '*Boom*' before turning back to the counter. "Hold the cheese," she said and turned to Chrisna, "You don't object to meat, do you?"

Chrisna grinned. "No, I'm an Afrikaner. Meat is practically our staple food."

The woman picked up two small paper bags, placed

the pastries in them, and put the bags and two napkins on the counter.

Zenelda reached for the pouch hanging near her hip, but Chrisna stopped her. "Let me get this," Chrisna said, pulling her wallet from her purse and paying the woman.

They hadn't left the shop yet before both of them took a bite of their food. The croissant was soft and the meat had a smoky taste. She liked the flavor.

"Thanks," Zenelda mumbled as she chewed.

Once again, they stepped onto the sidewalk and headed down the street again, chatting about this and that.

Zenelda stopped in front of a display window. "Ooh, a sale!" she swooned, peering through the window at the large selection of shoes. On the window, a yellow dot displayed the words '*Soldes -70%*'. "We'll have to come back here," she said. "But first we need some striking outfits."

The next store was a clothing store and Zenelda stopped, took the last bite of her second pastry, and crumpled the paper bag in her hands. "Let's go in here."

Chrisna looked at her half-eaten croissant and took a large bite.

"No rush, I'll wait for you to finish," Zenelda said and threw the crumpled paper into a nearby green garbage bag, hanging from a green metal stand. She wiped her hands on the paper napkin, rolled it up, and tossed it like a basketball through the hoop.

"No, it's fine," Chrisna said and pushed the croissant

deep into the bag, folding the top over, and pushing it into her purse. Wiping her hands on the napkin, she said, "Let's go," and threw it into the bin.

When they entered, Zenelda hurried to look through the clothes hanging from several standing rails in the middle of the shop, but Chrisna slowly passed by the outer rails against the walls.

Colorful dresses covered the majority of the space. There were floor-length, knee-length, and mini dresses, with straps and without straps.

"I like this place," Zenelda said, holding up a flowy white knee-length dress with a bright red floral design.

"I like that," Chrisna said and smiled. "But I thought you said no floral dresses for tonight."

Zenelda grinned. "I know. We're picking out the clothes we're going to wear now, first, and this one's for me." She lifted another dress. "*This* is for you."

Chrisna gaped at the short powder-blue mini dress with the spaghetti straps. "You're *not* serious."

Zenelda forced a frown. "Do I look not-serious?"

"No." Chrisna sulked.

"I think *Kristal* would look great in this."

Looking at the dress for a moment, Chrisna took a deep breath, stepped forward, and took it from Zenelda. "Fine," she said with a mystical smile. "*Kristal* will try it on."

Three hours later, they stepped out of the last store. They

had brand new underwear on, and Chrisna felt a little uncomfortable in the tight material of her dress. However, *she* wasn't wearing it, *Kristal* was. She pulled down on the hem that pulled up above her knees, and Zenelda glared at her.

"Don't you dare," Zenelda admonished. "Stop fidgeting, you look amazing."

Zenelda wore the floral dress, a silver headband, and array of silver bangles, and flat red sandals with flowers on them. In one hand, she carried their old clothes in a large blue bag, but still wore her small pouch with the leather tassels. In the other bag, she carried more clothes, an assortment of accessories, and expensive make-up.

Chrisna carried a bag with their eveningwear in one hand and their shoes in the other. Glancing down at the silver strappy wedges on her feet, she looked at the second toe on her left foot with the small silver toe ring around it, and then looked up again. She felt tall.

"Do you wanna get some coffee?" Zenelda asked, stopping next to a restaurant with a large maroon awning and dark wood-paneled walls.

"Sure," Chrisna agreed, her feet aching.

They entered the restaurant and sat down on the wooden chairs matching the small round table near the window.

"We need to do something about your hair," Zenelda said as she put the bags down on the floor and inspected Chrisna's appearance.

Chrisna wrapped her fingers around her ponytail and

pulled out the band. The strands fell onto her shoulders, and she shook her head before straightening it with her fingers. "Better?" she asked, as she repositioned her glasses on the bridge of her nose.

"A little." Zenelda smiled.

The waiter brought their menus, and Chrisna looked at the items, but Zenelda just stared at her. "So," Zenelda started, "how blind are you?"

"What?"

"Can you see at all without your glasses?"

Chrisna peered over her menu and frowned, slightly offended. "Why?"

"I don't think *Kristal* wears glasses," Zenelda smirked.

"I do have contacts but I prefer not to wear them."

Zenelda gaped at her. "You have contacts? Why didn't you say so?"

The waiter took their order, and Chrisna pushed the salt- and pepper shakers around on the table, trying to avoid Zenelda's stare. "What?" she finally asked.

"Can I see your glasses for a second?"

Chrisna handed them to Zenelda, who squinted as she peered through the lenses. "You have to have great vision to be able to see through these."

"Funny," Chrisna sassed and held out her hand, waiting for Zenelda to give her glasses back to her.

"I don't think so," Zenelda declared, grinning mischievously. "I hope for your sake you have your contacts in your purse, because you're not getting these back."

She folded the arms over the lenses and pushed her hand underneath the table.

"Okay, that's not funny. Please give them back."

Zenelda shook her head. "Nope."

"I'm serious, give them back."

"Don't you trust me?" Zenelda countered.

"Not while you're holding my glasses hostage."

Zenelda beamed and handed the glasses back to her.

Surprised that she felt a little disappointed about getting them back so easily, Chrisna looked at the blue-rim glasses. "Okay," she conceded. "I'll put in the contacts." She placed her glasses on her nose, reached down, picked up her purse off the floor, and stood up, pulling down on the hem of her dress.

Zenelda gaped at her. "You're going to do it now?"

"Do you want me to change my mind?"

"Definitely not."

Chrisna took her purse as she left the table and headed to the small corridor with the sign '*La Toilette*' above the entrance. She walked over to one of the sinks, placed her purse on the rim, and washed her hands. After drying them thoroughly, she looked in the mirror and blushed when she saw how good she looked in her new dress.

Remembering the brief back and forth she had with Zenelda about paying for her clothes, she again felt guilty about how expensive it was. When she'd converted the Euros to Rands, she was shocked to realize that it would've cost her at least a month and half's salary for only her outfits.

She opened her bag and pulled out a small container from one of the compartments, opened it, and put it on the sink. Removing her glasses, she carefully put the contact lenses in and squinted a few times before looking in the mirror and smiling.

She pushed the large silver hooped earrings aside and brushed her hair before applying moisturizer, mascara, and lip-gloss.

While packing her purse, she glanced at her reflection one last time, and then left.

When she returned to the table, Zenelda's jaw dropped for a second, and then she cleared her throat. "Okay, I don't like it."

Chrisna sat down quickly. "You don't?" she quizzed as she absentmindedly touched her hair with one hand, and reaching for the compact mirror in her bag using the other.

"No. I don't want to be seen with you when you look that hot." She beamed.

Chrisna blushed and shifted her chair closer to the table.

Her coffee had arrived and she took a sip. "I do feel a little uncomfortable," she announced.

"The contact lens thing?" Zenelda asked.

Chrisna grimaced. "No, the new-look thing."

Zenelda smirked. "You'll get used to it."

Readjusting the straps of the dress, Chrisna shifted in her seat. "When?"

Eleven

Zenelda flung the bags on the bed in Chrisna's hotel room, heaving a sigh as she sat down on the couch near the window.

Chrisna placed her purse on the desk before removing their eveningwear from the bags, and hanging the dresses in the closet. Returning to the desk, she pulled her cell phone out of her purse and pressed the unlock button. The battery icon was still halfway full but she plugged it into the charger anyway, not knowing when she'll be able to charge it again.

"What time is it?" Zenelda asked.

Chrisna touched the skin on her bare left wrist for a second, and then checked her phone. "One-thirty," she said.

"We only have to meet up with Tyce at nine. So what do you wanna do until we have to start beautifying ourselves?"

Chrisna sat down on the bed, facing Zenelda, and replied, good-naturedly. "Well, before you completely disrupted my itinerary, I had planned on seeing some sights." Her phone beeped three times as the messages came through and she stood up, walked over to the desk again, and checked her phone.

"Who's stalking you?" Zenelda asked.

Reading the messages, she typed the replies as she spoke, "They're from my mom, asking if I'm having fun and telling me that my dad is constantly asking when I'm coming home. And she says that the church fundraiser went well."

"Sounds like you're close with your parents," Zenelda commented.

Chrisna sighed and glanced up before continuing to type. "Yes. My dad can be a little overprotective at times but my mom and I am very close. I guess it's because I don't have any brothers or sisters."

"I have three brothers and two sisters," Zenelda said. "But I haven't seen them since I left home."

Chrisna glanced up. "Don't you miss them?"

"They're all much older than I am. I'm the youngest by twelve years."

"So you haven't had any contact with your family for…" Chrisna paused and did the math. "For twenty-four years?"

"It's been that long?" Zenelda jeered, a pained expression on her face, as she touched her palm to her forehead. "Wow, I'm getting old."

Chrisna smiled as she looked down to her phone again. "Sandra wants to know how I'm doing and she's complaining because I'm not updating her." She typed again. "Oh, and she wants me to send pictures."

"Have you taken any?"

Chrisna smirked. "Not any normal ones. Most of them are of that party I can't remember."

Zenelda jumped to her feet. "Ooh, you have to show me those."

After a few more taps she finished typing the last message, pressed send and looked up at Zenelda. "I don't know, maybe later."

Grinning, Zenelda took a step forward. "Now you *have* to show me."

Chrisna sighed, pressed the gallery button, and scrolled to the photographs taken on the boat, before handing the phone to Zenelda and flopping down on the couch.

With the phone still attached to the charger, Zenelda leaned against the desk and scrolled through the photos. Every now and again, she'd make an '*ooh*' sound. "It looks like you had a blast," she said and continued scrolling, but a few seconds later, she looked up and gaped at Chrisna. "You kissed Tyce?"

Chrisna blushed. "A little."

"Why didn't you tell me?"

"I only found out last night."

Zenelda gave her a look that she couldn't quite understand.

"What?" Chrisna asked.

"So he knows you kissed him?"

Chrisna smiled. "*He* does. I'm the one who can't remember doing it."

"Then you have to wait."

"For what?"

"For him to kiss *you*." Zenelda grinned. "It's *his* turn."

Chrisna sighed. "He won't. Since I told him that I just wanted to be friends, he's been more than a gentleman about it."

"What do you mean?"

"Well," Chrisna's cheeks burned, "there were a couple of times that I thought he might, but he didn't."

"Do you want him to?"

Chrisna smiled shyly. "Maybe," she lied and looked down at her hands, twirling her wedding ring around her finger. "I don't know."

Locking the phone, Zenelda unplugged it from the charger, dropped it into Chrisna's purse, and walked over to the couch, stretching out her hands. "Come on, we need to go take some *normal* photos of you."

Just before 6pm, they were back at the hotel room, and while Zenelda took a shower, Chrisna sent Sandra a few of the photographs they had taken. There were about twenty photos of her walking down the street, sitting in front of a café eating the rest of her croissant that she'd put in her purse earlier, and standing in front of the Louvre. She'd posed in front of the glass pyramid at the Louvre, pointed at the St Jacques Tower and stood underneath a Metro sign. On the Pont d'Arcole Bridge, she'd leaned over the side, and she'd posed in front of the Notre Dame. Zenelda had commented on the dark clouds accumulating overhead and then reminded her of *number four* on her To-do list, *Dance the Tango in the rain in front of the Notre Dame*, but she'd merely shrugged it off. The last photo showed her eating a crêpe that they'd bought at a stand on their way back to the hotel.

Sitting down on the couch, Chrisna waited for Zenelda to finish, and when she exited the bathroom with the hotel towel wrapped around her body, she asked, "May I use your hairbrush?"

"Sure, it's on the sink," Chrisna said. "I never asked if we should go to your place to get some of your things. Where are you staying?"

"Here and there," Zenelda said. "I left my stuff at a friend's place where I spent the other night. I'll go there to get it eventually."

Chrisna frowned. "Do you have a place to stay?"

"I have many. I'm kind of couch-surfing. You know, whichever way the wind blows me." Zenelda returned to the bathroom, leaving the door ajar.

Chrisna's phone beeped, and looking at the message from Sandra, she giggled. "Sandra wants to know what happened to me, but she likes the new look," Chrisna said loudly. "And she's wondering who took the photos I sent her."

"Tell her," Zenelda yelled from the bathroom, "that you've changed your name, kissed a famous musician, and that you're touring Paris with a crazy woman."

Chrisna laughed. "She'll have a heart attack."

It had taken the taxi about fifteen minutes to turn onto Rue Oberkampf. It was already dark outside, unlike the previous nights, when it would still be bright daylight at nine o' clock. Looking up at the sky through the backseat window, Chrisna stared at the dark clouds.

They stopped in front of a large gray brick building with a purple neon 'X' on the front. Chrisna took a deep breath, and Zenelda handed her a tube of lipstick. Taking the lipstick, she pulled off the cap, leaned forward to look in the rearview mirror, and touched up her bright red lips. Her hand trembled a little.

Zenelda had helped her with her makeup, and she didn't recognize herself with the BB cream that gave her skin a healthy glow, the blush that accentuated her cheekbones, and the dark eyeliner and eye shadow that made her eyes look smoky.

Handing the lipstick back to Zenelda, she glanced through the backseat window, breathing in quickly when she saw Tyce standing in front of the entrance, dressed in a dark gray suit, black collar shirt with a gray tie, black wingtip dress shoes, and a black fedora with a gray band around it.

Chrisna realized too late that Zenelda had paid the taxi driver already and was now opening her door for her.

She took another deep breath, gripped her black

clutch purse in her right hand and stepped out of the car as Tyce hurried toward them.

He stopped a few feet away and gaped at Chrisna, dressed in a fitted black sweetheart-cut dress that reached up halfway above her knees, showing off her firm, well-proportioned body and long, shapely legs to perfection.

Zenelda had showed her how to put her hair into a French roll using the silver fork-clip they'd bought that afternoon, and the updo showed off her dangling silver earrings with the small clear stones at the ends.

Tyce stared at her, not moving, and it made her uncomfortable. She looked down, lifted the left high heel of her black stilettos a fraction, and glanced at the thin silver ankle bracelet with the tiny clear stone hanging from it.

"Stunning, isn't she?" Zenelda said and startled Tyce out of his trance.

He beamed and Chrisna's cheeks heated.

"You don't look too bad yourself," Zenelda said to Tyce.

It took him a second to look away from Chrisna at Zenelda. "Me? What about *you*?"

Zenelda curtsied and twirled around twice in her off-the-shoulder silver ankle length dress with the slit that reached up to her left knee, silver stiletto sandals, and a small silver-studded bright-orange purse that matched her amber-stone necklace and teardrop earrings.

"Shall we?" Tyce said and stepped in between the two of them with his elbows bent.

Chrisna grinned, and they both laced their arms through Tyce's as he led them to the door.

When they reached the red rope barrier, the bouncer merely nodded and unclasped the rope, letting them through. Chrisna glanced back at the long line of people queuing to get in as they stepped through the large steel door.

Inside, loud music filled the building as hordes of people danced, talked, and drank on all three levels of the club, draped in soft purple light. A few people greeted Tyce when they passed by, and Chrisna felt self-conscious at the way some of the men peered appreciatively at her as they passed around the outer perimeter and headed up a metal staircase.

Zenelda let go of Tyce's arm and rushed up the steps but Chrisna held on, afraid that she might trip in her high heels. Tyce looked at her, his soft, intimate gaze disarming as a breath caught in Chrisna's throat. He smiled knowingly, pulled her arm out of his, and took her hand.

When they reached the third floor, Chrisna peered over the steel railing at the ground floor, designed in the shape of an 'X'. Purple leather couches, stools, and high neon glass tables stood in the gaps around the X-shaped dance floor where a DJ mixed his songs on a large glass turntable. Chrisna looked at the second and third levels with their similar steel railings on the opposite side of the club.

Tyce gripped her hand tighter and pulled her away

from the railing toward a glass cubicle with thick purple curtains, drawn back and hanging in the corners.

A large man, dressed in a black tuxedo, opened the pivot glass door and let them in.

The noise level dropped considerably when the door closed, and Chrisna glanced around the space filled with purple leather couches, glass coffee tables, and a bright neon bar counter with two bartenders, dressed in white dress shirts, mixing drinks. A group of four women sat in one corner, drinking pink liquid from martini glasses, and opposite them, two couples were ordering drinks from a waitress dressed in a tight black cocktail dress with a white squared apron tied around her waist. Everyone looked exquisitely groomed, and Chrisna inwardly thanked Zenelda for telling her that she couldn't wear her summer dress.

Tyce stopped near the far left corner where Zenelda had already made herself comfortable on the short part of the L-shaped couch. Chrisna sat down on her left near the corner, placing her purse between her and Zenelda.

"What would you like to drink?" Tyce asked.

"I'll have a Martinez," Zenelda said.

"Surprise me," Chrisna said, and Tyce grinned before he left.

"Way to go, *Kristal*," Zenelda said and smiled.

Chrisna grinned and shifted in her seat, trying to pull down the hem of her dress.

"Stop fidgeting." Zenelda frowned. "*Kristal* doesn't fidget."

Pushing herself back on the couch, Chrisna pressed her knees together and placed her hands in her lap.

A few seconds later, Tyce returned, took off his jacket, placed it on the armrest, before sitting down next to Chrisna, leaving a considerable gap between them. "The waitress will bring the drinks," he said and stared at Chrisna again. "Did you throw your glasses in the Seine again?" He teased.

"Again?" Zenelda frowned.

Chrisna crinkled her nose as a naughty smile spread over her face for a second before she smiled at Zenelda, flushing. "Did you see that photo where I leaned over the railing of the boat, holding onto my glasses?"

"Yes."

"Well," She cleared her throat, "apparently, I threw them in the water shortly after that."

"Why?" Zenelda quizzed. "Not that I care, you should've gotten rid of them a long time ago. But why?"

"I have no idea," Chrisna confessed, smiling beatifically.

Zenelda looked at Tyce, who merely shrugged, a lop-sided grin playing on the right corner of his mouth.

"It sounds like I missed one hell of a party."

Chrisna smiled at Tyce, and he returned her smile.

"Ere zou go," the waitress said in a thick French accent and placed the round silver tray on the coffee table in front of them. "One Martinez," she said, raising a martini glass with a bright orange liquid and placing it in front of Zenelda when she raised her hand. "One Blue

Fizz." She raised a tumbler glass with a blue milky liquid.

"That's for her," Tyce said and pointed to Chrisna.

The waitress placed the drink in front of her, and she looked at the milky liquid, hoping that it wouldn't actually taste like milk.

"And a Privateer," the waitress said and placed the tall glass of orange liquid, filled to the rim with ice, and garnished with a strawberry, in front of Tyce.

"Thank you," he said and handed her money.

Chrisna couldn't see how much he had given her, but the waitress smiled broadly before she left.

Zenelda raised her glass and held it up. "What should we toast to?"

Tyce raised his glass and glanced at Chrisna, who took her glass and said, "To new beginnings." She clinked each of their glasses and took a sip. The drink had a sweet-sour taste and she recognized the gin but it wasn't too strong or milky at all. She liked it.

"You didn't look me in the eyes when you toasted," Zenelda said. "That's bad luck. You're gonna have terrible sex for the rest of your life."

Chrisna choked on her drink and pushed her hand in front of her mouth, coughing a few times before she glared at Zenelda.

"Are you okay?" Tyce asked, looking concerned.

"She will be." Zenelda grinned. "But she'll have to kiss someone in the next minute to void the curse."

Chrisna gaped at Zenelda and then glanced at Tyce, who was giving Zenelda a fierce look.

Putting down her glass on the table, Chrisna sighed. "Okay." She stood up, straightened her dress, leaned down, grabbed Zenelda's face, and planted a kiss on her lips.

Zenelda gaped at her when Chrisna stepped back, sat down again, and casually took another sip of her drink.

Tyce clapped his hands a few times. "Brilliant," he guffawed.

It took Zenelda a few seconds to come out of her trance but then she smiled. "Still surprising me, *Kristal*," she said and took a sip.

The music amplified for a few seconds when the glass door opened, and Chrisna looked up at the couple entering. The woman had a black shoulder length hairstyle and she looked to be in her sixties, elegantly dressed in a tight fitting, dark dress that covered her knees, a gold three-quarter jacket, black pumps, and a gold clutch purse. She glided in on the arm of a much younger man, who looked to be still in his twenties. He wore a black and white tuxedo with a black bowtie, which made him look uncomfortable.

"Kristal. Darling!" the woman called and walked toward them.

Chrisna nearly choked on her drink again and she glanced at Zenelda, who raised her eyebrows.

"Fancy seeing you here," the woman said as she stopped near the couch. She spoke in an aristocratic English accent, and it reminded Chrisna of how the actors used to speak in old British films.

Tyce jumped up and stretched out his hand. "Good evening, Mrs. Wooten," he said, and Chrisna frowned.

The woman looked at his hand and then up at him. It didn't seem like she recognized him. Gently placing her hand in his, he shook it and then stepped aside to offer her his seat. She sat down next to Chrisna, and her escort sat down on the other side of her. Zenelda shifted closer to Chrisna, and Tyce sat down on Zenelda's right.

"How have you been, dear?" Mrs. Wooten asked Chrisna.

"Fine," Chrisna said, shifting uncomfortably.

"Oh, where are my manners?" Mrs. Wooten said and smiled a skew smile. "This is Eudo, he doesn't speak any English." She pointed to her escort.

"I'm Zenelda," Zenelda introduced herself as she leaned over the table, holding out her hand. Mrs. Wooten frowned, gently placed her hand in hers, and Zenelda shook it, almost violently. "Nice to meet ya."

"And you are?" Mrs. Wooten asked, looking at Tyce.

He forced a smile. "Tyce Turcotte, ma'am. We met at the party on the boat the other night. You were kind enough to have your driver take Kristal and me back to our hotels."

Zenelda glanced at Chrisna, who shrugged.

"Of course," Mrs. Wooten said and turned to Chrisna, taking her left hand and looking down at her wedding ring. "I see you still haven't been able to get rid of it."

Chrisna glanced at Tyce, and she couldn't read his

expression. Pulling her hand out of Mrs. Wooten's hold, she placed it on the couch next to her left thigh, hiding the ring. "Not yet," she said, looking at Mrs. Wooten.

The woman smiled her skew smile again. "Do it as soon as possible, I say." She looked at Zenelda and Tyce. "When *she* told me about how she wanted to throw her ring off the Eiffel Tower, I thought it was a fantastic idea. My Albert ran off with his harlot ten years ago, and the first thing I did was to melt my wedding ring into a coin. I carried it around for many years, reminding myself that I was stronger than my circumstances."

Chrisna gaped at Mrs. Wooten and then glanced at Zenelda, who slowly grinned.

"After hearing her story," Mrs. Wooten continued, "I gave her the coin." She elegantly pushed her hair over her shoulder with the tip of her middle finger. "I don't need it anymore." She glanced at Eudo. "I'm satisfied with my life now."

Zenelda shifted forward on the couch. "What do the engravings mean?" she asked intrigued.

"Well," Mrs. Wooten said and her face lit up. "The eight-point star means harmony, balance, and regeneration, and the daisies symbolize simplicity and patience."

Zenelda looked at Chrisna. "That's pretty much what Leverette said." She shifted back in her seat again.

"Thank you," Chrisna said, still a little taken aback.

"You're very welcome, dear." Mrs. Wooten glanced at Eudo, who stood up and helped her to her feet.

Tyce jumped to his feet. "Wouldn't you like to join

us for a drink?"

Mrs. Wooten smiled her skew smile for the third time, and said, "No thank you. You kids have fun."

Chrisna watched as Eudo and Mrs. Wooten sat down on a small couch near the entrance, and seconds later, the waitress approached them.

"Boom," Zenelda almost whispered.

"Epic boom," Chrisna said and took a huge gulp of her drink.

Zenelda jumped up. "Who would like to dance?"

"What?" Chrisna asked, still staring at Mrs. Wooten.

"This is a club, isn't it?" Zenelda asked. "And I'm pretty sure that the synonym for '*club*' is '*dance*'."

"No, thanks," Chrisna said and looked up at Zenelda. "I can't really dance to this music. I can '*Sokkie*', but I haven't done that in years."

Zenelda raised her eyebrows. "What's '*Sokkie*'?"

Chrisna searched her mind for a second and then said, "It's an Afrikaner dance. I can't really explain it."

"Tyce?" Zenelda asked.

He frowned. "*I* don't know what '*Sokkie*' is."

Zenelda's bubbly laugh echoed in the room. "No, I'm asking if you wanna dance."

"Oh. No. Not right now, thanks."

Chrisna wasn't sure but she thought Tyce looked annoyed.

"Suit yourselves. Mama's gonna throw it down," Zenelda said and left.

A few seconds of silence followed after they'd

watched Zenelda shimmy out the door.

"I'm sorry," Chrisna finally said.

Tyce frowned. "What for?"

She forced a grin. "I'm not sure exactly, but you look upset."

He took a sip of his drink and leaned back in the couch. "No, I'm fine."

She didn't believe him. "Is that a real '*fine*' or a '*sometimes fine*'?

Grinning, he sat up again and turned to look into her eyes, pulling his left knee onto the cushion, and putting his arm on the back of the couch. "It's an '*I think you look amazing*' '*fine*'."

She blushed and struggled to force back her grin. "Thanks," Chrisna said. "I think you look amazing too, even with the gangster-hat."

He frowned. "You don't like it?"

"No, its fine," she lied.

"Is that a real '*fine*'?" He grinned.

"It's an '*I think you can wear a tiara and still look good*', '*fine*'."

He laughed a deep, throaty laugh as he shifted closer to her, removed his hat and placed it on her head. "Okay." He cleared his throat. "Then *you* make it look sexy."

She gripped the rim of the hat with her right hand, turned her left shoulder toward him, and leaned her chin on her collarbone, puckering her lips. "Like this?"

"*That* you shouldn't do," he said.

She frowned, lifted her head, squared her shoulders, and removed the hat. "Does it look that bad?"

He smiled. "No, it looks *that* good."

Chrisna's cheeks burned and she handed the hat back to him. He placed it on the table, and casually pushed his fingers through his hair, straightening it.

She smiled as she watched him tuck the left side in behind his ear before leaning back. "What?" he asked.

"Nothing." She sipped on her drink and glanced at Mrs. Wooten straightening Eudo's bowtie.

"They do make a lovely couple, don't they?" Tyce teased.

"Like *Harold and Maude*," Chrisna said and grinned.

"Now that's a great film. Do you like old movies?"

She nodded. "*Dr. Strangelove* is my favorite."

He grinned. "*Or how I learned to stop—*"

"*Worrying and love the bomb.*" She snickered.

He shifted closer to her again and his knee almost touched her knee. "Okay, what's your all-time favorite movie?"

"Wow," she said. "That's a tough one. There are so many."

"What pops into your head?"

Chrisna grinned when the only movie she could think of at that moment was *Zack and Miri makes a Porno*. It was one of the most recent movies Sandra had made her watch.

"What?"

"Nothing," she said. "What's *your* favorite movie?"

"I want to say something masculine like *The Godfather* or *Apocalypse Now*," he said, "but that would be a lie."

Chrisna shifted forward on the couch and the spot where her knee touched his, heated up. She leaned forward with her elbows on her knees. "What is it?"

He rubbed the back of his neck. "*The Princess Bride*."

"Really?"

He nodded, looking embarrassed.

Chrisna put her hand on his knee. "I love that movie."

Tyce beamed as he placed his hand on top of hers, and a shiver ran down her spine. "Do you have a favorite song?" he asked.

She breathed in slowly. "*Trying on the World*."

Tyce let go of her hand and shifted back in his seat. "That's not fair."

She pulled her hand back and sat up straight. "Why not?"

He sighed deeply and then suddenly looked serious as he tucked his hair back behind his ear. "I don't want to do this anymore," he said. "I thought I could but it's too hard."

"Do what?"

"This," he said. "Us."

Chrisna's heart skipped another beat as she glanced down. "I'm not sure what you mean," she lied.

"You say you just want to be friends but you don't really, do you?"

"Of course I want us to be friends."

"Are you sure that's *all* you want?"

Her heart stuck in her throat and she couldn't answer, even if she wanted to.

"Spend one night with me," he pleaded.

"What?"

He leaned forward again. "Spend one night with me. A night you *can* remember," he said. "And if you still want to be just friends after that, then I'll be *just* your friend."

She couldn't hide her shock and he must've noticed.

"I'm not talking about having sex," he backtracked quickly, and she felt like she couldn't breathe when he leaned over and took her hand. "Spend tonight with me?"

She was trapped in his eyes. "Okay." The word slipped out before she could stop herself.

Tyce smiled, stood up, and pulled her to her feet. "Come on."

Chrisna reached for her purse and saw the silver-studded orange purse on the couch. She picked it up. "Wait, what about Zenelda?"

Taking Zenelda's purse from her, he said, "Don't worry, she'll understand." He let go of her hand, picked up his hat, walked over to one of the bartenders, said something to him, and the man took the purse and his hat, pushing it in underneath the counter.

He returned to Chrisna, stopped next to the couch, lifted his jacket off the armrest and put it on. He smiled again, and then held out his hand.

Chrisna took a deep breath. 'Okay, *Kristal.* You're in charge,' she thought to herself and took his hand.

Twelve

When they stepped out of the club, Tyce stopped and turned to Chrisna. "Do you trust me?"

Her head was spinning and this time she couldn't blame it on the alcohol or the marijuana. "Yes," she said and she meant it.

He smiled. "Then I have one request."

"What is it?" she asked, but what she actually felt like saying was '*sure, anything*'.

"While you're out with me, you can't say no."

Her heart skipped a beat. She breathed in and exhaled slowly before answering, "Okay, but then I have one request also."

"Anything," he said.

She grinned. "*You* can't say no either."

"Deal." He squeezed her hand and returned her grin.

"I also have a request," Zenelda said loudly, and they turned to see her standing a few feet away with her arms folded.

"Zenelda," Chrisna said and let go of Tyce's hand. "I'm sorry, I didn't think—"

"I was just about to head upstairs again," Zenelda

said, "when I saw you two sneaking out."

"We weren't sneaking," Tyce retorted.

"Then where are you running off to?"

Tyce walked over to Zenelda, whispered something in her ear, and then she smiled.

"Okay, then," Zenelda said. "I was coming to tell you guys that I ran into some old friends anyway. Carry on. Have fun!"

"Are you sure?" Chrisna asked.

"Absolutely," Zenelda said and turned around, heading to the door.

"What was your request?" Tyce asked.

Zenelda stopped, turned around again, and approached them. "Oh, yes. I want you guys to promise me something."

"What?" Chrisna asked.

"That you won't kiss each other tonight."

"What?" Tyce gaped at her.

Zenelda smiled. "I heard your little pact about not being able to say no, so you can't say no to me now."

"Wait a second," Tyce said. "That doesn't—"

"She's right," Chrisna said and forced a grin. "We should've specified the details of the deal a little more clearly."

"Listen to her," Zenelda laughed. "She's very particular about details."

Feeling almost relieved about the pressure being taken off, Chrisna said, "We promise," and looked up at Tyce. "Right?"

He sighed. "Okay, fine."

Chrisna liked that he looked disappointed about not being able to kiss her, and then he looked at her with a wide grin. "Do you think you'll be able to control yourself?"

She grinned. "You just worry about yourself, *Casanova*."

"Okay, I have some floor to burn. You two have fun now." Zenelda grinned mischievously and walked over to Chrisna, hugging her tightly, and whispering in her ear, "You'll thank me tomorrow."

"We'll see," Chrisna said when she pulled out of the hug.

"I'll walk you in," Tyce said when Zenelda stepped back and headed to the door again. He turned to Chrisna. "I'll be back in a second."

Zenelda took Tyce's arm and they walked through the large door.

When he returned less than a minute later, Chrisna raised her eyebrows when she saw the black motorcycle helmet in his hand.

"I originally thought that we should go for a walk but since I can't kiss you, I'll have to get your heart racing another way. Are you ready to have some fun?" he asked and took her hand again.

She shook her head from side to side. "Yes."

They walked down the street, turned left at the corner, passed a bar with orange walls and painted blue cracks, and Tyce stopped next to his metallic black motorcycle, parked on the side of the road. He placed the helmet on the seat and removed his jacket, holding it out to her. "Put this on."

"I'm not cold."

"Please."

She turned around, clenching her purse between her knees, and pushed her arms through the sleeves.

He grinned as she turned back to face him and took a step closer. His hand brushed her neck, sending shivers down her spine as he straightened the collar of the jacket and fastened the buttons.

With every movement of his hands, she trembled a little, and she already regretted her promise to Zenelda.

When he was done, he stepped back and picked up the helmet. "You'll have to wear this as well," he said.

"Don't *you* need one?"

"I only have the one but I'll drive carefully, promise."

"I don't think we should make any more hasty promises tonight." Looking at the helmet in his hands, she sighed. "But, okay." Clasping her hair-clip between her fingers, she pulled on it and her locks fell to her shoulders. Quickly placing the clip in her purse, she pushed her fingers through her hair, and looked up at him.

He smiled and then slowly pushed the helmet over her head, fastening the strap under her chin and closing the visor.

Pushing the bike upright, he flung his leg over the seat and kicked the stand, so it retracted, and then he held out his hand to her. "Get on."

Chrisna hesitated as she glanced over the large motorcycle.

"You can't say no, remember." He smiled.

Forcing a smile, Chrisna looked down at her tight short dress and then looked up at Tyce again. "Don't look," she said, her voice muffled beneath the visor. She pulled her dress up as far as it would go without exposing herself, took his hand, stepped on the footrest, and threw her left leg over the seat. Pushing the dress down between her thighs, she grabbed onto the back of his shirt as she tried to keep her balance.

"Are you ready?" he asked.

She wanted to scream '*no!*' but she'd promised not to use that word. So she whispered, "Nee." instead.

Tyce started the engine, and Chrisna gripped her purse tightly. She felt his strong muscles move beneath the fabric of his shirt as she wrapped her arms around his waist. The motorcycle roared, vibrating underneath her, and Chrisna closed her eyes when the bike thrust forward, holding onto Tyce's torso just a little tighter.

"You okay?" he shouted.

She opened her eyes. "I'm fine!"

The wind pushed against her body and she looked at the buildings and the lights blurring past them. He turned left at the next street, and she tightened her grip when the motorcycle tipped. She had to remind herself that she wasn't in South Africa as they drove down the right side of the road.

When they turned onto a long street, he sped up,

and her heart leaped into her throat.

Slowing down a few minutes later, he turned left into a narrow street, let go of the left handle, and placed his hand over hers, squeezing gently. She gasped. "Don't do that!" she yelled, and he let go, grabbing the handle again. Chrisna felt his body shake and she blushed, realizing that he was laughing at her.

The tar road turned to bricks as they crossed a bridge, and she glanced at the concrete bank with the row of thin green trees outlining the river, and the lights reflecting on the water.

The street narrowed again and the tall buildings on either side, towered over them. A few seconds later, Tyce slowed down considerably, pulled off the road at the edge of another bridge onto a broad sidewalk, and stopped.

Switching off the engine, he put his hands over hers and pulled them apart. "This is our stop," he said, and she sighed.

Gripping his hand tightly, she put her weight onto the left footrest and pulled her right leg over the seat, almost losing her balance as she stepped onto the ground.

Letting go of her hand, he pulled the kickstand out with his foot, slipped off the seat, and slowly leaned the bike onto the stand.

"So," he said, turning to face her. "Did you like it?"

Her heart raced as she looked up at him through the visor. "Well, I can't say *no*."

He grinned and carefully removed the helmet.

She wasn't sure if the tingling she felt was from the bike's vibrations or from his closeness, but she struggled to control her breathing.

He pushed a strand of hair out of her face, and a shiver shot through her body.

"What?" she asked when she noticed his amused sideways grin.

"Well, you don't have helmet hair, but..." he started.

Walking to the bike, she leaned forward and looked at herself in the side mirror. Her hair looked a mess. She pushed her fingers through the strands and straightened them. "Better?" she asked when she turned back to face him.

He grinned again. "Well, I can't say *no*."

She hit him on the arm with her purse, and he flinched. She smiled. "So what are we doing here?"

"You'll see," he said and took her hand, leading her back in the direction they'd come from, but after they'd crossed the street, he turned left.

She liked the way her hand felt in his and she liked the way his jacket smelled of sandalwood. He glanced at her and smiled. She liked the way he smiled. No, she loved the way he smiled at *her*.

Tyce stopped in front of a small supermarket, and placed the helmet on the ground. He turned to her, undid the top two buttons of his jacket, and pushed his hand into the inside breast pocket. He didn't touch her but he might as well have. She trembled and breathed in sharply.

Pulling out a small leather wallet, he opened it, handed her a Twenty Euro bill, and pushed the wallet into his pants pocket.

"What's this for?" she asked, looking at the money.

He grinned, picked up the helmet, took her hand again, and pulled her into the store, stopping in front of the first aisle. "Buy something, anything, and then meet me out front when you're done."

Chrisna frowned. "What am I supposed to buy?"

"Something fun, surprise me," he said and hurried down the aisle.

Chrisna looked at the money in her hand, sighed, and then browsed the aisles. She stopped in front of a large selection of children's toys. Toys are fun, aren't they? She grinned.

Having no idea what Tyce had in mind, she picked up a pack of playing cards and looked at the price, €2.99. Did Tyce want her to spend all the money?

She walked further down the aisle and a small box of colored chalk caught her eye. She couldn't imagine what they'd do with it but she picked it up anyway, €1.48, and walked to the counter and paid.

She glanced around but couldn't see Tyce. "Au revoir," the woman said and handed her the change.

Chrisna tried to copy the way the women said goodbye, but she knew she'd gotten it wrong. She smiled anyway, picked up the bag, went outside, and saw Tyce holding a bag in one hand and his helmet in the other.

"What did you get?" he asked when she reached him.

Handing the change to him, she smiled. "That depends on what you have in mind."

Looking at the money in his hand, he frowned. "You didn't spend much."

"You're disappointed that I didn't spend enough of your money?"

He smiled, pushed the change into his pocket and took her hand again, leading her back toward the bike.

Just opposite the motorcycle, there was a small alcove in the bridge wall which created a viewing space over the river, and that's where Tyce stopped.

He let go of her hand, placed the bag and the helmet on the ground against the wall, before taking her purse from her and placing it in underneath the helmet. Reaching into a supermarket bag, he pulled out a box with two wine glasses, opened it and handed her one.

She put the supermarket bag that she was still clutching down, and took the glass.

Placing his glass on the ground, he pushed the empty box back into the bag and pulled out a bottle of wine. Turning the cap, he smiled. "You drink red wine, right?"

She nodded as she held out her glass.

Wrapping his hand around hers, he poured the dark red liquid into the glass and she was sure he could feel her hand tremble. He let go, filled his own glass before putting the bottle down and holding up his glass. "Here's to the people who make toasts," he said.

Chrisna grinned, looked him straight in the eyes, clinked her glass against his, and took a sip. "That's good," she said.

"Not bad for a €4 bottle of wine, right?" he said and turned, placing his glass on the ledge and leaning over to look at the water.

Chrisna also placed her glass on the ledge, took off Tyce's jacket, folded it neatly, and positioned it on top of the helmet.

"Are you hot?" Tyce asked when he looked at her.

She grinned. "I must be, otherwise you wouldn't have insisted that I spend the night with you." She couldn't believe the words that were coming out of her mouth. Was she becoming Kristal? *Chrisna* would never dream of saying something like that to guy.

He looked up, smiled, turned his back to the wall, and pushed himself up, sitting on the ledge. "Hey, I liked you before you turned into *this*." He glanced over her body and picked up his glass.

She took a sip of her wine and stared at the beautiful reflections of the lights on the water. "Why?"

"Why what?"

"Why did you like me?"

"You mean besides the fact that I think you're kind, interesting, strong, funny, and beautiful?"

She blushed, looked up at him, and then grinned. "Yes, besides that."

"When we were sitting at La Fosse, you said something that caught my attention, and I knew you were different."

"What did I say?" she asked intrigued and turned to

face him.

He grinned. "I'll tell you when you're ready to hear it."

"That's not fair," she said.

"I know." He kicked his legs back and forth and took another sip. "So what did you buy?"

Placing her glass on the ledge again, she reached down and picked up her bag of goodies. "Close your eyes and pick something," she said, holding the bag out to him.

He closed his eyes, pushed his hand into the bag, pulled out the box of chalk, and opened his eyes again. "You bought chalk?" he asked, grinning.

"What did you expect me to buy?"

"I didn't expect anything," he said.

"Then you can't be disappointed."

"I'm not. You did actually buy *anything*." Tyce smiled as he jumped to the ground, and reached into his pocket. He pulled out his cell phone, and pressed a few buttons until the flashlight on the back came on.

"What are you doing?"

"I'm going to draw a mural," he said and placed the phone face down on the ground. Opening the box of chalk, he took out the white one, and went down on his knees in front of the wall. "Be the lookout, will you?"

"Are you serious?"

"Hey, you bought the chalk," he chortled and started drawing.

Chrisna picked up her glass, took a step forward so as

to block him from view and watched the people passing over the bridge.

She could hear the chalk scratching against the wall and she asked, "What are you drawing?"

"You," he said. "But you can't look until it's finished."

She smiled at a couple of passersby who glanced in her direction. "Are you done yet?" she asked moments later.

"Almost. I want to get your features just right."

"Did you study art in school?" she asked.

"No," he said, and she heard the chalk scratching against the wall a few more times before he said, "Okay, all done. You can look now."

When she turned around, Tyce was sitting on the ledge again, swinging his legs back and forth, as he sipped on his wine. She looked down at where the phone lit the wall and she smiled. If it wasn't for the long hair, the cartoonish drawing could've just as easily have been of a man, with its red half-moon for the mouth, straight white line for the nose, and two oval shapes with blue circles in them for the eyes.

"Uncanny," she deadpanned.

"I know." He smiled and held out the box of chalk to her. "Your turn."

Taking a sip, she placed the glass on the ledge, took the white piece of chalk, and handed the box back to Tyce.

Crouching down, she pressed her knees together and

pushed against the wall with one hand to try to keep her balance. She scratched the chalk against the wall a few times and then stood up. "All done," she said.

"*That* was fast."

"I'm *that* good," she offered and smiled.

Tyce jumped to the ground, stepped back, and rubbed his chin, contemplatively. "Hmmm...You've captured me perfectly," he said as he looked at the stick figure drawing. "You'll have to sign it."

Stepping forward, she bent down and started writing, 'C-H-R-I...', and then she stopped, scratched over the writing, and wrote '*KRISTAL*' underneath it.

She handed Tyce the chalk, and he wrote, '*TYCE*' on the wall but then thought better of it. He scratched it out, and underneath it wrote, 'CASANOVA'.

Chrisna chuckled, and then she felt a raindrop graze her eyelash and fall on her cheek. She looked up, and another drop fell on her face, and another. Within a few seconds, the rain poured down.

"Let's go," Tyce said, and she rushed to help him pack up everything and shove it all – including her purse – into one bag. She shrugged into his jacket, pushed the helmet over her head and fastened the strap. Tyce lend her a hand in getting onto the bike.

Chrisna placed the bag in between her and Tyce, and she held onto his waist as they drove back over the river.

Tyce zigzagged through the traffic and, about ten minutes later, he parked on the side of the road near a cream-colored five-storey building with black awnings over the twenty-odd small balconies.

Helping her down, he parked the bike, took the bag from her, and grabbed her hand as they raced to the entrance; Stopping only long enough for a man dressed in a black suit, holding an umbrella, to push the gold handles on the glass door to let them in.

When they stepped into the lobby, Chrisna stopped, struggling to loosen the helmet's strap.

Tyce pulled her hands away, quickly undid the strap and lifted the helmet off her head.

Pushing her hair out of her face, she looked down at the puddle they were making on the black-marble floor.

Tyce tipped her head up. "Let's get you out of those clothes," he said and took her hand again.

Chrisna's heart raced and it wasn't because of the motorcycle or the short distance they'd run to the hotel. She squeezed his hand and held on tightly to his arm, partly because she was trying not to slip on her wet high heels, but mostly because she loved the feel of his closeness.

As they walked toward the shiny gold elevators, they passed a black-marble reception desk with a gold water-wall behind it. Chrisna glanced up at the two large glass chandeliers hanging from the black and gold patterned ceiling, emitting soft yellow light.

When they reached the elevator, the door was already open and a man, dressed in a white long-sleeved collar shirt with a black waistcoat and white gloves, stood inside.

Stepping in, the operator glanced at them before pulling his shoulders back and looking in front of him again.

"Five, please," Tyce said.

The operator pushed the button and the door closed.

"So, you sing in elevators?" Tyce asked a few seconds later.

She smiled. "Only when I get stuck."

He grinned mischievously.

"Don't even think about it," she said.

The door opened and, stepping out, Tyce led her through the narrow corridor with the black carpeting and stopped at the third door.

Letting go of her hand reluctantly, he pulled his wallet from his pocket, opened it and pulled out a black key card, swiping it through the lock. The light turned green and he opened the door.

When Chrisna entered, the lights came on automatically, and she glanced around the room. It was big. Not rock-star-big like she'd seen in the movies, but big enough to have a large black L-shaped couch in the middle of the gold carpet, pointing at a flat screen TV that hung from a wall mounting. A black glass coffee table filled the space in between. Behind the couch, there was a glass dining table with four black high-back chairs, a black-marble top kitchen counter on her left, and three high rectangular-paneled windows with four gold curtains hanging on the sides. Behind the coffee table, three small steps led up to a large glass-paneled wall that stretched across the width of the room, and she could see a bed on the other side of it.

Tyce pulled on the shoulders of his jacket, and she jumped.

"May I take your jacket, miss?" he asked in a formal tone.

She smiled, pulled the soaked jacket off her shoulders, and handed it to him.

Taking it, Tyce pushed the hair in behind her left ear, and she breathed in quickly.

"You should change," he said.

She chortled. "Why? I thought you liked me just as I am."

He smiled, stepped back, walked to the glass-paneled wall, pushed on it, and opened a door.

Chrisna took off her wet shoes, left them on the floor near the couch, and walked to one of the windows. Rain splashed onto the balcony as people in the street below rushed to their destinations, attempting to avoid getting too wet.

"Here you go," Tyce suddenly sounded behind her, and she turned around.

He walked down the steps toward her, holding onto a clear squared bag and when he stopped in front of her, she saw that the bag held her blue camisole and the other items she wore to the concert.

"You had my clothes dry cleaned?" she marveled at his thoughtfulness.

"There's a bathroom through there." He smiled and

pointed to where he came from. "Leave your clothes in the tub. I'll send it out tomorrow."

"Thanks," she said, took the bag from him, and walked to the room, glancing at the queen-sized bed with the black covers as she passed by.

The bathroom had the same black and gold color scheme. Chrisna placed the bag on the small counter top next to the sink. She undressed, bundling her dress around her underwear before placing the wet clothes in the tub. Opening the bag, she took out the camisole, black jeans, and underwear, and put them on. She checked her makeup in the mirror. Aside from the blush that had washed off, her makeup still looked surprisingly good and she was grateful that Zenelda had insisted that they buy the expensive stuff.

Taking off the silver dangle earrings, she placed them on the countertop, pushed her fingers through her damp hair, and returned to the living room.

Tyce sat on the couch with his back to her. His bare feet rested on the coffee table next to the bottle of red wine and two filled glasses.

When she rounded the couch, she saw that he had changed into a dry pair of blue jeans and a dark gray t-shirt with the Blades of Blue signature printed in white on the front.

"I love your shirt," she said and smiled.

He returned her smile, took his feet off the table and sat up. "You can have it," he said and pulled the t-shirt over his head, flinging it at her.

Catching the shirt, she marveled at his smooth, toned upper body with a black tribal tattoo covering his right side from his hip to just underneath his arm. "Thanks," she said, not just referring to the shirt. "But I think you'd better put it back on."

"Are you sure?" he asked.

She nodded and threw the shirt back at him, exhaling slowly when he pulled it over his defined abs, resisting the urge to move closer and touch them and…

"I found this in the bag," Tyce broke her train of thought as he reached into his pants pocket, pulling out a packet of playing cards.

Chrisna stepped past him and sat down on the couch, leaving a gap between them. "You said I should buy something fun," she said, picking up one of the wine glasses and taking a sip.

"So you like games?" he asked, arching his eyebrows and turning to face her, pulling his left knee onto the couch.

Grinning, she said, "Card games, yes." She took the packet from him, opened it and pulled out the cards. "You want to play?"

He grinned. "Sure, I want to play, but I have something else in mind." He reached over and brushed his fingers over her wrist as he took the cards from her.

She trembled and inhaled sharply.

Shuffling the cards, Tyce split the deck and handed her one of the halves. "Turn the cards face down, take one from the top and put it down here, face up," he said, pointing to a spot on the cushion between them.

She did as he asked and placed a Deuce on the cushion.

"Okay," he said. "What are your *two* favorite places in the entire world?"

Chrisna didn't have to think for too long before answering. "There's this big tree near the Riet River, just outside of Jacobsdal, where I sometimes go to read when I want to be alone."

"Sounds nice," he said.

"It is. In the winter the reeds have this golden glow when the sun shines through them."

Chrisna couldn't quite read his expression.

She shifted backward, leaned against the back of the couch and turned her head to look at him. "And the other place would have to be the house I grew up in, I guess."

He frowned. "Okay, but I did say anywhere in the world."

She twirled the ends of a few damp strands of hair between her fingers. "Well, I've never been anywhere really, except Cape Town. This is the first time I've traveled to another country."

"It is?" He looked surprised. "Wow."

"Ja, okay. Your turn," she said.

Flipping the top card over, Tyce placed a Four on top of her card. "Let me have it," he said.

Thinking for a moment, she turned her body toward him, pulling her right knee onto the cushion, mirroring the way he sat, and said, "Name *four* things that you're afraid of."

He rubbed the back of his neck. "Spiders..." he answered sheepishly.

Chrisna giggled, and then pushed her hand in front of her mouth. "Skees."

He narrowed his eyes. "It's a legitimate phobia," he said. "So is going to the dentist."

"I'm with you on that one."

His expression suddenly turned serious. "I guess I'm afraid that people won't like my songs."

"You don't have to be afraid of that," she exclaimed, giving him an encouraging smile.

He forced a grin. "And four..." He held up four fingers. "Never getting the chance to kiss you, I guess."

Her heart skipped a beat and she swallowed.

"Your turn," he said.

Chrisna looked at the cards in her hand and then looked up at him again. "Wait, we *have* kissed."

"*You* kissed *me*, it doesn't count."

She frowned. "You didn't kiss me back?"

"Does it matter? You can't remember it anyway."

"I guess not," she sighed and flipped her card over, placing an Ace on top of the Four.

He smiled. "Tell me *eleven* things you like about me."

"Eleven?"

"Yes, an Ace counts as eleven."

"No, it doesn't," she said. "An Ace is *one*."

"Fine." He sighed, stretching his arm across the back of the couch. "Tell me *one* thing you like about me."

She grinned. "I like your body."

He frowned, trying to hide his amusement. "That's it?"

"Let me finish," she said, placing her pack of cards on the coffee table and taking a big sip of wine for courage before looking at him again. "I like your hair, and the way you sometimes tuck it in behind your ear. I like the way you rub the back of your neck when you're uncomfortable or nervous."

He smiled shyly.

"I like the way your smile touches your eyes," she continued, "and the warmth in your voice when you laugh. I like your arms, and the way you held me when you hugged me, the way you held me when you wanted to throw me in that fountain, and when I woke up in your arms in the trailer. I like the way you smell, and how your scent lingers on your clothes. I like how I feel completely safe when I'm with you, and I like the way my hand feels in yours." She lifted her arm onto the back of the couch and pushed her fingers in between his. "I like your eyes, and the way they light up when you're excited about something, and how I could see the disappointment in them when Zenelda said that you couldn't kiss me. But most of all, I like the way you look at *me*."

Tyce breathed in deeply, and without looking away, he placed his cards on the coffee table, let go of her hand, and leaned forward.

"What are you doing?" she asked softly.

The closer he came, the farther she leaned back, until her back pressed against the armrest, and he leaned over her with his face a few inches from hers.

"You know we can't," she whispered as her heart pounded against her chest.

Leaning on his right hand that pushed on the cushion next to her shoulder, he stood with his right foot on the floor, and his left knee pressed down between her knees. Lifting his left hand, he pushed a strand of her hair out of her face.

She shivered, lifted her hand, and pushed his hair in behind his left ear.

He closed his eyes and slowly breathed in.

She took a deep breath, pushed against his chest and sat up. "Let's go," she said.

He opened his eyes. "Where are we going?"

"You're taking me to the Notre Dame."

Thirteen

The rain streamed down her body when Tyce helped her off the bike. He'd parked in between a few small trees on the sidewalk opposite the Notre Dame.

Taking his hand, she pulled him across the street and onto the brick-paved square.

Before they'd left the hotel, Tyce had given her another pair of flip-flops, blue this time, and he'd put on trainers. He'd changed into a plain black t-shirt because he'd said that he didn't want to ruin *her* Blades of Blue shirt, and although he'd offered her another one of his jackets, she'd declined because it wasn't cold at all, or perhaps she just didn't feel it.

"What are we doing here?" Tyce asked when they stopped in the middle of the almost empty square, with the Notre Dame Cathedral towering over them.

"Dance with me," she said, squinting as the rain fell on her face.

"What?"

She stepped closer to him and took his other hand. "It is number four on my list."

"What list?"

"A list of five things I have to do while I'm in Paris," she smiled. "Zenelda gave it to me."

He arched his eyebrows. "And dancing in the rain is on that list?"

"More specifically," she said, "dancing the Tango in the rain in front of the Notre Dame."

He grinned. "That *is* specific. What else is on the list?"

"I've hugged the Venus de Milo, I sang in front of people, but the list says it has to be at least fifty people and there were only about twenty in the elevator," she said. "And then there's *'Get a mime to talk'*, but the only mime I've met scared me a little. So I'm attempting the Tango now and would appreciate your help."

He frowned. "That's only four. What's the fifth one?"

"I'll tell you when you're ready to hear it." She smiled coyly and winked at him.

He smiled back as he raised her right hand and placed his arm around her waist, pulling her tightly against him. Looking down at her, he sang, *"Pum pa rum pum, parararara..."* He stretched her right arm out, twisting his body to the left, as he led her across the bricks and continued to sing. *"Pum pa rum pum, parararara..."*

On the last *'ra'*, he stopped, dipped her backward, leaned over her, and looked serious as he stared into her eyes.

Her breath caught in her chest.

Pulling her up slowly, he wrapped his arms around her waist and tightened his grip so that her body pressed against him. He pressed his face into the side of her neck, and she finally took a breath again, wrapped her arms around his shoulders and leaned her head against his chest. They swayed slowly as the rain streamed down their bodies.

"Are you cold?" he whispered, and she felt his warm breath on her neck.

"No," she said and trembled.

"You're not supposed to say '*no*'."

She smiled. "Then yes, I'm not cold."

With her ear pressed against his chest, she could feel his heart racing, and even though his shirt was soaking wet, she felt the warmth of his body against hers.

He lifted his hand, ran his fingers up and down her spine near the small of her back, and she trembled again, tightening her arms around his neck.

The bells of the cathedral started ringing, and they stepped in time with the rhythm of the chimes.

When she heard the twelfth chime, she stopped moving, pulled away from him, lifted her head, and brushed her fingers over his cheek before tucking his hair in behind his ear. He breathed in deeply, and she ran her fingers around his neck, pushed herself up onto the balls of her feet, and pulled his face down to hers.

"We can't." He breathed in, stopping his lips an inch from hers.

She smiled. "It's after midnight. It's not *tonight* anymore."

Grinning, he let go of her waist, loosened her grip around his neck, and took a step back.

"What are you doing?" she asked, suddenly feeling rejected.

He looked at her without answering, and she took a step toward him, but he took a step back. She frowned and took another step, but he stepped back again.

"That's not funny," she said.

"You can't kiss me," he finally said, looking serious.

"What? Why not?"

"You've already done that."

She looked at him for a second, took a deep breath, and then grinned mischievously. "Then will *you* please kiss *me*?"

While smiling his perfect smile, he slowly closed the gap between them.

When he reached her, he placed his hands on her cheeks, and when he lowered his lips to meet hers, she closed her eyes and waited.

She could feel his breath on her face, but he didn't kiss her, and after a few more seconds, she opened her eyes again.

He smiled, "Do you have any idea how beautiful you are?" and then he closed his eyes and leaned in.

Closing her eyes again when his lips gently touched hers, her body numbed and she leaned into him, placing her hands on his chest. She felt him tremble when she opened her mouth a fraction, and he tenderly deepened the kiss.

Every inch of her body came alive as his lips moved over hers, and the heat surged through her. She didn't want the moment to end. It was perfect.

But then Tyce pulled back and let go of her face. She opened her eyes and saw the intense look in his perfect green eyes.

She smiled. "Do you have any idea how beautiful *you* are?"

The corners of his mouth curled up and he took a deep breath, but before he could exhale, she stepped closer, pushed her hand around the back of his neck, pulled him down to her, and kissed him, almost forceful-ly.

Pushing the door open with his shoulder, Tyce swung Chrisna around, and pushed her into his hotel room as he continued to kiss her.

Her hand gripped around the back of his neck as she pulled him down to her, and stepping backward, she almost tripped on the flip-flops, so she kicked them off as she stepped.

A moment later, the back of her legs hit the armrest of the couch, and she fell back onto the cushions, taking him down with her, giggling.

Tyce smiled at her for a second and then buried his face in her neck, kissing her just below her earlobe, drawing a line of kisses down her throat.

She pulled her head back and breathed in deeply when he kissed his way around her neck to the other ear. Her heart raced and her breathing became shallow as the heat burned through her limbs. She arched her back and moaned when he kissed the indentation between her collarbones. Her entire body tingled.

Gripping her wrists, he forced her arms above her head and pressed his lips down on hers again, kissing her with urgency. Pushing his fingers through hers, he pulled his face back, and she breathed in as he stared down at her.

Feeling like she couldn't move even if she wanted to, she looked into his eyes, which seemed a little darker somehow, and then she lifted her head to kiss him, but he pulled back, looking serious all of a sudden.

"We're not doing this," he said and pushed himself off her.

"What?"

He stood up and disappeared around the back of the couch.

Staring up at the black and gold patterned ceiling, she tried to control her breathing and thought about what had just happened. However, after a few moments of useless contemplation, she rolled off the couch, stood up, straightened her hair, and noticed that the door to the balcony was open.

Stopping in the doorway, she saw Tyce standing against the metal railing.

The rain had subsided and there was only a light

drizzle falling onto the balcony floor.

"What's wrong?" she asked.

He stared down at the street and didn't answer.

She took another few steps. "Tyce?"

He lifted his head but still didn't look at her. "I'm sorry," he said.

"For what?"

She noticed him tightening his hands around the railing, his knuckles white and his jaw clenched before he finally spoke again, "You're not ready."

"I'm not?" She stepped forward, her stomach a knot of anticipation and frustration.

He looked at her before answering forlornly. "No, you're not."

"What's going on?" Chrisna pleaded.

He pushed himself away from the railing and walked toward her, stopping about three feet away from her. "Give me your hand," he said.

Frowning, Chrisna lifted her right hand.

"No," he said, "the other one."

"What's wrong?" she asked again.

He reached down, took her left hand and turned it over, with her palm facing the ground. "This is what's wrong," he said, lifting her hand up so that she could see her wedding ring.

Her heart plummeted into her stomach and she pulled her hand back. "I'm sorry," she said, trying to swallow down the lump caught in her throat. "I'll take it off if you want."

When she looked up, his expression softened. "You shouldn't do it just to please me."

She looked down at her ring again. With every fiber of her being, she wished that she could pull the ring off her finger and throw it over the railing right then and there, but something was holding her back. "Are you angry with me?"

He pushed his fingers in underneath her chin, lifting her head. "I'm not," he said and then he leaned forward and placed a soft kiss on her forehead before pulling back again. He smiled but this time his smile didn't touch his eyes.

She forced a grin, pushed herself up onto the balls of her feet and gently pressed her lips against his for a few seconds before pulling back. "Will you sleep with me?"

His eyes briefly widened and then he frowned. "No."

She smiled. "I'm not talking about having sex. Besides, you're not allowed to say no."

Sighing deeply, he half-smiled, brushed a strand of hair out of her face, and then took her hand.

He led her back into the living room and up the steps to the bedroom, letting go of her hand once they were next to the bed, and then he opened the closet door. "I don't have another pair of sweatpants," he said while rummaging through the shelves.

Chrisna looked down at the Blades of Blue t-shirt he had left on the black covers, and then she picked it up and smelled his scent that lingered in the material.

"I have these," he said and turned around, holding

up a pair of long navy-blue pajama pants.

She quickly pulled the t-shirt away from her face. "Thanks," she said, took the pants from him, and went into the bathroom.

Placing her wet clothes in the tub, she took a quick shower and then dried her hair as best she could before pulling the Blades of Blue t-shirt over her head. Putting on the pajama pants, she pulled on the string to tighten the pants around her waist, before pulling down the shirt and rolling the legs up to her calves.

When she opened the door, Tyce was sitting on the bed with his guitar on his lap, picking at the strings.

Standing in the doorway, she looked at him for a while, and then softly said, "Your turn."

He looked up, grinned slowly and then stood up, placing the guitar on the bed. Lifting a black piece of clothing off the covers, he went into the bathroom, and then glanced at her once more before closing the door.

Chrisna walked around the foot of the bed to the right side, propped the pillow up, sat down with her back against the headboard, and pulled her knees up to her chest. She stared at her wedding ring. Was she really missing Werner? She knew she loved him. She would always love him. Why had it hurt her so much when she found out he was seeing someone else? Was it because she wanted him back?

Shrugging off the thought, she looked at Tyce's guitar. He was right, she wasn't ready, and she wasn't being fair to him. But all she wanted at that moment was for

Tyce to hold her. She couldn't remember the last time she'd just been held by someone who made her feel safe, who made her forget about everything else, except the moment, except him.

She leaned over, picked up the guitar, crossed her legs, and put it on her lap. Pressing the chords while strumming the strings, she hummed a few notes.

"Play me something," Tyce said, startling her.

He was standing in the bathroom door, dressed in only a pair of black boxer shorts, and Chrisna stared at his bare chest. "What?" she asked.

"Sing me a song in your language."

"You want me to sing?"

"Please," he said and sat down next to her on the bed. Leaning his back against the headboard, he stretched his legs out over the covers.

"I don't know," she said, feeling self-conscious.

Turning his head, he looked up at the ceiling and closed his eyes. "I won't look at you."

Watching him for a few seconds, she took a deep breath, looked down at the guitar, strummed the strings, and then played a few chords before singing the ballad. "*Dalk is net 'n vier-letter woord, 'n miskien vir eendag weggesteek. 'n Vraag na soeke reeds gevind. Vir my is jy net dalk.*" She looked at Tyce. "*Dalk, ja dalk is die eendag nou, miskien is net miskien vergete. 'n Gedagte sonder einde. Is jy vir my net dalk?*"

Halfway through the song, she felt her throat tightening up, and as she sang the line, "*Dalk is alles net 'n droom*", her voice cracked. She stopped and wiped the tears with the back of her hand before they could escape.

Tyce opened his eyes and looked at her. "Are you okay?"

She tried to swallow down the lump in her throat. "I'm fine. Sorry," she said and handed him the guitar.

He placed it on his lap and softly said, "That was beautiful. What does it mean?"

She leaned back against the headboard, pulled her knees up, and stared at the ceiling. "It's about '*maybe*', and how '*possibly*' is sometimes hidden away for '*one day*'. How we keep seeking for what we might already have found, and how that '*one day*' may be now." She frowned. "If I'm translating it correctly." Sighing, she continued, "How someone could be a '*maybe*' for someone else, but at the same time, *maybe* it's just a dream." She forced a grin. "Or something like that."

"That's kind of sad," Tyce said and picked at the strings of the guitar, playing a slow melody, "having to rely on '*maybe*'."

She twirled her ring around her finger a few times before sitting up. "Tyce?"

He stopped playing and looked at her.

"Will you hold me?" she asked.

Placing the guitar down on the floor beside the bed, Tyce reached up, pushed a switch on the wall above the nightstand, and the room went dark. He searched for her hand and finding it on her knee, he gently took it and pulled her closer to him. As he lay down on his back, he pulled her down, so her head rested on his chest. He wrapped his arms around her, holding her, and she sighed deeply, breathing in his scent.

She felt his chest moving up and down beneath her as his breathing slowed. And then she lifted her head, shifted up a fraction, and gently ran her fingers over his lips before leaning down and placing her lips on his.

When she pulled back, he sighed. "What was that for?"

"I just needed to," she said and shifted down again, placing her head on his chest.

He slowly stroked his fingers up and down her left arm, and she sighed deeply. As her body relaxed, a tear escaped and rolled down her cheek.

Chrisna woke up on her side with Tyce's arms wrapped around her, and she could feel his breath on her neck. The light from the living room flooded through the glass paneled-wall, and the bedroom seemed bigger somehow, less intimate than it had before. She breathed in deeply and slowly exhaled as she turned her body to face him. He stirred and opened his eyes. "Good morning."

"Morning," she whispered.

He lifted his head and kissed her on the forehead, letting his lips linger on her skin for a few seconds before he pulled back.

"What was that for?' she asked.

"I just needed to."

She sighed. "Will you take me back to my hotel?"

Leaning into Tyce, Chrisna held on around his waist as the motorcycle sped down the road. The ride didn't feel at all as exhilarating as it had before. It didn't feel like she was racing toward something, it felt like she was driving away from something that she didn't want to leave behind.

Tyce had given her his leather jacket to wear and, even though it was warm already, the thought of holding onto something of his made her accept it without arguing. She'd zipped it up before they left and pushed her purse in through the opening.

When they stopped in front of her hotel, she took a deep breath and held onto him for as long as possible, until he unclasped her hands and helped her off the bike.

As she stepped onto the ground, she looked up at him, not liking the way he looked back at her. His expression seemed indifferent.

She swallowed. "You can't be *just* my friend, can you?"

He breathed in. "I'm sorry."

Opening the zipper, she pulled her purse out, clenched it between her knees, and removed his jacket, holding it out to him. "Thank you," she said before taking her purse again.

He took the jacket without saying a word, and she lingered next to the bike for an awkward few seconds before walking to the entrance of the hotel. Opening the door, she stopped and turned around. "I mean it, thank you," she said loudly, and then walked through the door.

She hurried to the elevator and it took forever to open up. When she stepped in, the space felt smaller than usual, and as she waited to reach the fourth floor, she breathed in as deeply as she could before exhaling. She did that a few times, trying to get rid of the tight feeling in her chest, but it didn't work.

The flapping sound the flip-flops made as she walked to her room, irritated her, and she had to push the keycard into the slot three times before the door unlocked.

Turning around after closing the door, she jumped when she saw Zenelda sitting on the small couch by the window. "Where were you, young lady?" Zenelda asked and smiled. "It's almost…" She looked at her bare wrist. "Well, it's late." She glanced out the window. "Or early, I guess." Zenelda wore dark blue jeans, multi-colored wedges, and a bright orange fitted t-shirt with the words '*I was Jessie's Girl*' printed in white on the front.

"What are you doing here?" Chrisna asked. "How did you get in here?"

"Why are you upset? I just came to see how your night went, and when I found out you weren't back yet…" She smiled mischievously. "I sweet talked one of the cleaners to let me in."

Tossing her purse on the bed, Chrisna flopped down next to it. She sighed and kicked off the flip-flops.

"What are you wearing?" Zenelda gaped at her.

Pushing her hair out of her face, Chrisna sat up and looked down at the gray Blades of Blue t-shirt and pajama bottoms.

Shifting forward on the couch, Zenelda frowned. "You're not upset about me being here, are you? What happened?"

The lump pushed up her throat and her vision blurred as the tears formed in her eyes. "I don't want to talk about it," she said and wiped her eyes with the back of her hand.

"Did Tyce hurt you?"

"No." She fell back onto the bed and stared at the ceiling. "I hurt *him*."

There was a long pause before Zenelda asked, "He wants more than you think you can give him."

Chrisna turned her head and looked at Zenelda, sitting on the edge of the couch, leaning forward. "Yes."

Zenelda tapped her index finger against her forehead. "You're still thinking with this, aren't you?"

Turning onto her side, Chrisna rested her head on her elbow. "I don't know what's wrong with me." She sniffed.

The sympathy in Zenelda's eyes was obvious. "There's nothing wrong with you, sweetie."

"There has to be." She turned on her back again, staring at the ceiling. "You were right, Tyce is a good guy. I don't want to hurt him."

"How exactly will you be hurting him?"

"I don't know how to let Werner go."

"Do you want to?"

Raising her hand, she looked at her wedding ring. "I'd like to think that I do."

"Where is that coin Mrs. Wooten gave you?"

Chrisna looked at her and frowned. "In my purse in the closet. Why?"

"I have an idea," Zenelda said, stood up, and walked over to the closet, opening the door.

"What?" Chrisna asked, and it took a lot of effort for her to sit up.

Returning to the couch, Zenelda sat down again and opened her hand, showing Chrisna the coin. "We're gonna flip for them?"

"What?" Chrisna gaped at her.

"If the coin lands star-side up, that means you can never see Tyce again, and if it lands daisy-side up, then you can never see Werner again."

"You're crazy. I'm not doing this," Chrisna said and stood up, walking to the bathroom.

"One, two, three," Zenelda counted, and when Chrisna turned around, she saw the coin spinning through the air before Zenelda caught it, flipped it over on the back of her hand, and kept it closed with the other one.

"What did it land on?" Chrisna asked anxiously.

Zenelda smiled. "Which side do you *not* want to face up?"

Chrisna frowned. "What?"

"The moment it landed on my hand, which side were you afraid of seeing?"

Chrisna glanced at her ring and then looked up at Zenelda again. "The star."

Grinning, Zenelda tossed the coin on the bed. "Then it doesn't matter what it landed on, you have your answer. You are more afraid of never seeing Tyce again."

"It's not that simple."

"Oh, but it is. For that one millisecond, you were thinking with your heart and not that congested brain of yours."

"But you're trying to have me base my decision on fear," Chrisna said and walked over to the bed, picking up the coin, and looking at the engraving of the eight-point star. "I already know I'm afraid."

"That's your problem. You're afraid of losing something that you never really had in the first place."

For a second, Chrisna wasn't sure if Zenelda was talking about Werner or Tyce.

"What do *you* think you're afraid of?" Zenelda asked and leaned back in the couch.

Chrisna looked at her ring again. "Letting go."

"Why?"

She took a deep breath and looked at Zenelda. "Because maybe I was wrong, maybe I should've tried harder, maybe it was my fault that we drifted apart, that I've failed us. That I've wasted half my life trying to build something that doesn't matter anymore."

Zenelda grinned. "You don't want Werner back,

you're just afraid that the time with him never meant anything. Well, if it meant something to *you*, then it meant something." She shifted forward on the couch again. "Why did you leave him?"

Sitting down on the bed again, Chrisna placed her hands in her lap and twirled her ring around her finger. "I didn't."

"What?"

"He said that it wasn't working anymore, that *we* weren't working anymore." She didn't wipe away her tears this time.

"So it wasn't you who ended it?"

Before she could answer, her cell phone rang, and she looked at the black clutch purse on the bed. It rang again.

"Are you going to get that?" Zenelda asked.

Chrisna didn't answer. She just stared at the purse.

Zenelda stood up, walked over to the bed, picked up the purse, and took the phone out, looking at the display. "I think you need to answer it," she said and held the phone up to Chrisna.

Blinking a few times, Chrisna looked at the screen displaying '*Werner*' and she froze.

After another ring, Zenelda turned it around and wiped her finger across the screen before holding it up to her ear. "Hello," she said, and Chrisna jumped up, grabbed her phone, and went into the bathroom.

Fourteen

"Are you okay?" Zenelda asked when Chrisna opened the door almost half an hour later and stepped out of the bathroom.

"I'm fine," she said, stopping beside the bed, staring at her phone.

"That was your ex, right?"

"Yes."

"Well? What did he say?"

She looked at Zenelda. "He called to wish me a happy birthday."

"Ah hell! That's right, it's your birthday." Zenelda jumped up, rushed over to Chrisna, and hugged her tightly. "Happy thirtieth, sweetie."

When she let go, Chrisna smiled faintly. "Thanks."

Stepping back Zenelda frowned. "That's not all he said, is it?"

Chrisna shook her head. "No. We finally talked, really talked. And he said that he missed me and that he wants us to try again."

Zenelda gaped at her. "What? Doesn't he have a girlfriend?"

"He said that he broke it off with her because she wasn't me. He misses *me*."

"I want to say '*Boom*' but I don't think it's a strong enough word." Zenelda said, and then frowned. "Wait. You don't really look upset. You almost look happy. Why do you look happy? Are you going back to him?"

Chrisna took a deep breath before exhaling slowly. "I feel like I can breathe again. It's been a long time since I've felt like I could breathe."

"I'm happy for you," Zenelda said and forced a grin for a second before it turned into a frown again. "But you didn't answer my question. Have you decided to go back to him?"

Chrisna tossed her phone onto the bed, walked over to the couch, and sat down, looking up at Zenelda. "I asked him why *he* thinks that we got divorced, and he said that we weren't happy, that he didn't know how to make me happy anymore, but that things could be different, that he could change."

Zenelda sat down on the edge of the bed. "And what did you say?"

"That he shouldn't have to." She glanced at her ring and then looked up at Zenelda again. "I told him that I loved him just as he is."

Zenelda looked disappointed.

"And then I told him that I wanted him to be happy, but that I also don't know how to make him happy."

"And?" Zenelda asked, looking anxious.

"And that I know he loves me too."

"You're killing me here."

"I thought I'd be glad when he said that he wanted me back, but instead, I felt panicked about getting stuck in that life again."

Zenelda gaped at her.

"I want things to change. I need my life to change, and I'm the only who can do that. I know that now."

"So—"

"It's over." Chrisna smiled.

Zenelda jumped to her feet, threw her arms around Chrisna's neck, and squeezed.

"Hey! I just said that I can finally breathe again, so please don't suffocate me now."

"I think you made the right decision."

"Me too. I finally know that I'm not tied to him anymore," Chrisna said, and Zenelda held on a moment longer before letting go and stepping back. But Chrisna frowned when she saw the tears rolling down her cheeks. "Why are you crying?"

Zenelda turned her back to her. "I'm not."

"Well, there's no music playing, and I don't need you to cry for me. Are you happy?"

Zenelda turned around and the expression on her face surprised Chrisna. She stood up. "You're *not* happy. What's wrong?"

"No, I am happy for you." Zenelda sniffed and wiped the tears with the back of her hand. "It's just that there's something I haven't told you."

Chrisna took her hands and they sat down on the

edge of the bed. "Tell me."

Taking a deep breath, Zenelda said, "I didn't come to Paris for just the concert, and I'm not on a marital sabbatical."

"You're not?" Chrisna asked softly.

Zenelda sniffed again. "No. Joe died of a heart-attack four months ago."

"What?"

Looking down at her hands, Zenelda rubbed her thumb over the music bar tattoo on her left ring finger. "I found him lying on the floor in his study with his sheet music and his guitar next to him. I tried to save him. I tried to give him CPR, but it was too late. When the ambulance arrived, the paramedic told me that it was too late." She sniffed again. "I just sat down in his chair and watched as he lay lifeless on the floor. I couldn't move, I couldn't breathe. All I kept thinking was that I couldn't save him."

"I'm so sorry," Chrisna whispered and hugged her tightly.

"I came to Paris because this was where we met. I wanted to feel close to him again."

Chrisna pulled back and smiled sympathetically.

"But most of all I just wanted to pretend that I was on one of my yearly getaways again, and that when I got home, he would be there."

"I'm really sorry," Chrisna said.

"Seeing how happy you were just now about moving on, made me realize that I have to admit to myself that he is gone. I can't go on pretending anymore."

Chrisna leaned over, picked the coin up off the covers, took Zenelda's hand, and turned it over. "Here," she said and placed the coin on Zenelda's palm.

Zenelda looked at the coin. "I can't."

"I don't need it. You saved *me*." She smiled.

"I did?"

Chrisna nodded. "Besides, a great friend of mine once told me that it's bad luck to take back a gift after it's been given."

Zenelda sighed deeply and then wiped her eyes. "Thank you."

Leaning in, Chrisna gave her a lengthy hug before standing up and holding out her hand. "Come on."

"Where are we going?"

"We're going to celebrate our birthdays."

Zenelda frowned. "But it's not *my* birthday."

Chrisna grinned. "Isn't it?"

"Are we going to the festival?" Zenelda asked as Chrisna hurried down Rue Saint-Honoré.

"Just trust me," Chrisna said and gripped her purse tighter under her arm as she pushed through the horde.

Chrisna had taken a quick shower and then had to answer a couple of phone calls from her parents and Sandra, wishing her a happy birthday. She felt a little guilty about telling them that she was seeing all the sights, but telling them that she was having an unbelievable time, wasn't a lie. In between the calls, she'd dressed into a pair of faded jeans, a bright purple halter neck t-shirt, and blue ankle strap sandals Zenelda had bought for her. She'd quickly tied her hair into a ponytail and applied moisturizer, mascara, and lip-gloss.

"Where are we going?" Zenelda asked as Chrisna turned left on Rue Saint-Florentin.

"Right here," Chrisna said and stopped.

Zenelda gaped at her. "You're not serious," she said, looking at the tattoo stand.

"Do I look not-serious?" Chrisna smiled.

"You want to get a tattoo?"

Chrisna turned to the bulgy man with the shaved head. "*We* want to get a tattoo."

"Happy birthday," Zenelda said, raising her glass of red wine.

"And a happy birthday to you." Chrisna smiled and clinked her glass against Zenelda's.

"And to commemorating our revival," Zenelda said and clinked Chrisna's glass again. "I still can't believe you got a tattoo."

Chrisna looked at the bandage on her right wrist. "I can't believe I didn't cry like a baby. You didn't tell me it would hurt that much."

"Well, you didn't tell me that we were going to get matching tattoos." She smiled and held up her bandaged wrist.

Taking a sip of her red wine, Chrisna sighed deeply and sat back in her chair, looking at the people enjoying their Sunday lunch at the small tables with the red table-cloths.

"You look happy," Zenelda said.

"I feel…" Chrisna searched for the word she wanted to use but all she could come up with was '*free*', and it wasn't exactly right.

"Liberated?" Zenelda asked.

"Yes." Chrisna smiled. "Exactly." She pushed a strand of hair, which had come loose out of her ponytail, in behind her ear. "Let's cut my hair."

Zenelda almost choked on a sip of wine. "What?"

Chrisna leaned forward. "Come on. Don't stop me now."

Zenelda grinned. "Quoting Freddy won't help you. It's Sunday remember, the salons are closed."

Sighing, Chrisna leaned back in her chair again, staring pointedly into the other woman's eyes.

"Ah, hell," Zenelda conceded. "Like that's gonna stop us."

"Delrico, you're amazing," Zenelda said and applauded, then, turning to Chrisna, said, "You can look now."

Chrisna kept her eyes closed. "My head feels naked."

Zenelda snickered. "You did tell him to get rid of all the hair you don't need."

"How does it look?" Chrisna asked, still too afraid to

open her eyes.

"Well, let's just say, that I don't think I can call you 'Sweetie' anymore, *Kristal*."

Taking a deep breath, Chrisna slowly exhaled and then opened her eyes. She gasped.

"Vous regardez fabuleux!" Delrico shrieked, and Chrisna glanced at the dark skinned man with the black sleeveless shirt and short cut-off jeans.

"What did he say?" Chrisna asked.

Zenelda smiled. "He said that you look fabulous and I agree. Wow!"

Looking in the mirror, Chrisna stared at her short feather-cut platinum-blonde hair.

"Ses yeux regardent incroyable," Delrico gushed.

"Yes, her eyes do look amazing." Zenelda grinned.

"You really like it?" Chrisna asked, feeling extremely self-conscious.

"No," Zenelda said. "We absolutely love it." She turned to Delrico and squeezed him tightly. "You are the best, thanks for opening your salon for us."

"Yes, thank you," Chrisna said, pushed her fingers through the short strands, and then smiled. "I think I'm finally ready." She glanced at the mirror a final time and said to herself, "I think I could be a Kristal."

The orange twilight enveloped the entire city of Paris as Chrisna stared through the mesh-wire fence on the top deck of the Eiffel Tower.

Looking down, she couldn't see far enough over the edge, but she knew the garden with the pond in between the trees had to be somewhere beneath her. Taking a deep breath, she pulled the ring off her finger and held it up between her right index- and middle fingers. "Maybe I should just pawn it," Chrisna said and looked at Zenelda, who leaned against a gold-plated telescope.

"Maybe you should." Zenelda grinned.

Chrisna smiled, and then pulled her hand back over her shoulder. "But where's the fun in that?" She catapulted her arm forward, flinging the ring through the diamond-shaped wires, and watched as it fell to the ground. "Boom!"

Fifteen

"What's in the bag?" Zenelda asked.

"You're very inquisitive today. Don't you trust me?" Kristal pushed through the hordes of people streaming down Rue Saint-Florentin.

"I do, but why didn't you want me to see what you bought at that Supermarket?"

"Real trust should never have a '*but*' in it."

Zenelda smiled. "I am liking this new, take-charge, you."

It had been dark for a while, and the last night of the festival was in full swing. Kristal stopped when they'd reached the end of the street and she saw the crowds of people gathered in the square, listening to whoever was performing on stage.

"Where did you meet Joe?" Kristal asked loudly, trying to raise her voice over the music.

Zenelda frowned. "Why?"

"You're not going to make this easy for me, are you?"

Grinning, Zenelda pointed in a south-westerly direction. "There, on the far right of the stage, just across the street. There's a statue of a man and a horse."

Kristal gripped the paper bag in her one hand and tightly squeezed her purse under her other arm. "Then that's where we're heading."

They pushed through the people and Kristal never said '*skees*' once. When they reached the edge of the crowd, they crossed the street on the far right side of the stage. There were two identical statues mirroring one another on either corner of the street, but Zenelda led her to the left one and stopped just behind it.

Kristal looked up at the tall square brick pedestal with the rearing horse and a naked man with, what looked like, a quiver hanging from his back. It appeared as if the man was trying to calm the horse.

"Here," Zenelda said, standing on the north side of the statue.

Kristal walked over to her, placed the bag on the ground, and pulled out a large white pillar candle that she placed near the foot of the pedestal, and then she took out a box of matches. Pushing the paper bag into her purse, she took a match from the box and struck it. Bending down, she lit the candle before blowing out the match.

"Tell me how you met," Kristal asked.

Zenelda frowned and then looked at the candle. She took a deep breath. "It was July, exactly fifteen years ago. It was a Friday night, around six. I remember because *Iron Army* was due to open the concert at seven, and I had just had this huge fight with the lead singer about not wanting to go to his trailer before they went on stage." She didn't take her eyes off the candle. "I stormed off and ended up wandering in this direction. But then I heard the most incredible melody and found Joe standing right here, playing his guitar. I stood a few feet away, watching him for some time as the people just rushed past him. They didn't get that they were missing something remarkable."

A lump formed in Kristal's throat as she listened to the loving tone in Zenelda's voice.

"Eventually, the concert started and he stopped playing." Zenelda continued, "He took the few coins from his guitar case, walked over to me, and asked if he could buy me a cup of coffee. I think that was the point of no return. It was only later that he told me that he was a well-known songwriter from London and that he enjoyed playing on the street because it was the best way to test out his material."

Kristal tried to swallow down the lump, and Zenelda looked up, tears lingering in her eyes.

"He would've liked you," Zenelda said.

Kristal grinned. "You think so?"

Nodding, Zenelda took Kristal's hand and said, "You are inspiring."

Kristal smiled. "So are you."

"There's one other thing I haven't told you," Zenelda said, and Kristal looked apprehensively at her. "Remember the daughter I didn't have?"

"Yes."

"Well, Kristal's the name I would've given her."

She gaped at Zenelda. "So that's where you got my name from?"

"Yes, I'm sorry. I just didn't know how to explain it to you."

Kristal smiled again. "I'm honored."

Zenelda grinned, squeezed her hand, and then she let go, kneeling down next to the candle. "You drive me crazy," she said and blew out the flame.

Standing up, she wiped her eyes with the back of her hand, straightened her shoulders, and cleared her throat. "So how do you want to spend the rest of your birthday?"

Grinning, Kristal reached into her purse. "Well, I still have these," she said and held up the two backstage passes she'd picked up in the trailer.

Zenelda gaped at her. "You took those?"

"I thought you might want one as a souvenir."

"Brilliant," Zenelda said and took one from her, pulling the string over her head.

As they neared the stage, Kristal stopped.

"What is it?"

"I think I recognize the singer," Kristal said and listened for a few moments before hurrying through the crowd to where she could see the stage. "I don't believe it."

"What!?" Zenelda yelled.

Pulling her phone from her purse, Kristal tapped the

screen and then held the phone up so Zenelda could see the video recording. "Look!"

"Boom!" Zenelda yelled. "Do you know who that is?"

"Yes, he's the guy from the elevator."

"That's Marshall Lovette."

Kristal frowned. "Who?"

"He used to be the lead singer of *Falcon Heart*."

"Who?"

Zenelda sighed. "They sang that song, '*Another Year of Thunder*'."

Kristal gaped at her. "No way, everybody knows that song."

Zenelda grinned. "He hasn't recorded anything in decades. I thought he ran a used car dealership or something."

"Come on," Kristal said and hurried to the side of the stage, holding her backstage pass up as she stopped in front of the two guards. "Hurry, Zee!" she yelled, waving Zenelda over.

Stepping through the gate, Zenelda asked, "Did you just call me Zee?"

"What? You're the only one who can give out names?"

When they stopped in front of the second two guards, Kristal raised her pass again and then said, "We want to go up." She pointed to the stage.

One of the guards escorted them up some steps at the back of the structure.

"That was easy," Zenelda said as they hurried up the steps.

A man, dressed in black and wearing a radio-headset, met them at the top of the steps, and directed them to a spot on the side near the front of the stage. Kristal's heart pounded against her chest when she caught a glimpse of the sea of people.

She looked at Zenelda and mouthed '*Boom*'.

Zenelda smiled and mouthed back, '*Happy birthday*'.

Watching the man with the bushy hair, thick beard, and silver-rimmed glasses, sitting on a high chair in front of the microphone stand, Kristal listened to the slow melody as he sang, and the crowd cheered when he finished.

"Thank you," he said, picked up a small water bottle that stood on the floor next to his chair, looked in Kristal's direction, and waved the bottle in the air.

Kristal glanced back at the man with the radio-headset, who was busy yelling at another man, also dressed in black. Looking at the bottles of water on the table next to them, she grinned, handed Zenelda her purse, and picked up one of the bottles before walking onto the stage. Glancing back, she saw Zenelda blocking the man with the radio-headset as he tried to pass her.

"Well, who do we have here?" Marshall Lovette asked, his voice echoing.

Kristal could merely force a grin as she handed him the water and turned around, heading off the stage.

"Hold up there, sweetheart." She heard his voice

echo again and she stopped. "At least give the crowd a wave."

Turning around, she looked at the thousands of people watching her, and she raised her trembling hand.

Most of the crowd waved back at her, and her heart skipped a beat.

"Come here for a second," Marshall Lovette said and waved her over.

Her heart raced as she approached him.

"What's your name?" he asked.

She kept her eyes on him, trying not to look at the crowd again. "Kristal," she almost whispered.

"Kristal," he repeated and his voice resonated in her ears. "What a beautiful name. Well, thank you for the water, Kristal."

She smiled. "You're welcome and thank *you* for singing in the elevator."

"Hold up, folks. What a coincidence. This girl was trapped with me in the elevator of the Eiffel Tower two days ago."

"Yes," she said, "but you wouldn't remember me. I had glasses and a brown ponytail then."

He frowned and then pushed his hand over the microphone, leaning in her direction. "You're the girl who was standing next to me?"

She nodded.

He smiled. "Just wait there a second." Removing his hand from the microphone, he looked at the crowd again. "I was going to wait to do this song but now is as good a time as any," he said. "Could I get another mic on stage please?"

She froze and watched as another man, dressed in black, run onto the stage and handed her a microphone before Marshall Lovette said something to him and he left.

"Come stand here next to me," he said, and she hurried to his side. Placing his hand over his microphone again, he said to her, "I'm sure you know this one."

As the music started playing again, the crowd went wild, and her body numbed. It felt like she was standing in the crowd looking at herself.

Marshall Lovette started singing, and she glanced at Zenelda, who was clapping her hands together above her head. Lifting the mic to her mouth, Kristal softly sang with him. And when she looked at him, he smiled, and then she couldn't help but belt out the chorus. "*I know that you know that we had to say goodbye. And you know that I know that our love will never die. But there are no tears on Forgotten Avenue, and there are no years but the years I've known with you. But I left you in wonder, and we both know, it's gonna be another year of thunder.*"

She let him sing the parts she couldn't quite remember, but most of the time, she confidently sang along. At the parts where only music was playing, she turned while clapping her hands above her head, and the crowd clapped with her. During the last chorus, the entire audience was singing along, and when the song ended, they went wild.

Marshall Lovette smiled and then stood up while applauding in her direction. He reached into his pocket, and then leaned in to the microphone. "Kristal, everybody!"

Her heart leaped into her throat when she realized that the crowd was cheering for her.

Stepping out from behind the mic, he hugged her briefly before pushing something into her hand.

She frowned and looked down at the seven Euros fifty in her hand.

"That was amazing," Zenelda yelled and flung her arms around Kristal's neck when she stepped off the stage. "When I wrote more than fifty people on the list, I didn't mean three hundred thousand."

Kristal couldn't stop grinning, and when Zenelda let go, she opened her hand and looked at the money. "Can I buy you a cup of coffee?"

Zenelda grinned, and Kristal turned around, watching Marshall Lovette sing his last song, and then he took a bow, leaned in to the microphone and belted out, "Ladies and gentlemen, Blades of Blue!"

Zenelda flopped down on the bed in the hotel room and stared at the ceiling, grinning from ear to ear. "Now, *that* was epic," she said, glancing at Kristal, who lingered by the door. "What's wrong?" she asked.

"I have to go."

Sitting up, Zenelda frowned. "It's three o'clock in

the morning."

Kristal knocked on the door twice, and then waited while tightly gripping her purse under her arm.

Zenelda had called a taxi from the room phone, and luckily Kristal could remember the name of the hotel. She smiled when she left her hotel, she smiled the entire seven minutes it had taken for the taxi to drive to Rue Duphot, and she smiled when she realized how close the hotel was to Place de la Concorde.

Forcing her smile back, she knocked again, and the door opened.

"Hi," she said.

Tyce gaped at her. "Your hair."

She pushed her fingers through the short strands. "Oh, yes. I kind of had a haircut."

"Kind of?" His mouth stayed open as he stared at her.

"Anyway, I'm sorry I woke you," she said.

It took a few seconds for him to reply. "I wasn't sleeping."

She looked at his blue jeans and the bright yellow t-shirt that turned his eyes an intense shade of green as he stood barefoot on the gold carpet.

"How've you been?" he asked.

"Good," she said, trying to keep from smiling. "How've *you* been?"

He rubbed the back of his neck. "Good."

She cleared her throat. "Did I leave my earrings here?"

He frowned. "You came over at this hour for your earrings?"

"Yes." She tried to look as serious as possible. "They're very expensive. Did I leave them here?"

"Yes, you left them in the bathroom," he mumbled, looking defeated. "I'll go get them, and your clothes." Leaving the door ajar, he disappeared around the corner.

Kristal stepped into the room, softly closing the door behind her, and waited next to the couch for Tyce to come out of the bedroom.

He stopped for a second on the outside of the glass door and looked at her. "I'm sorry I couldn't find a better bag," he said and then he descended the steps.

She looked at the bag in his hand. It was one of the bags they'd received at the supermarket the day before. Tyce stopped in front of her and held the bag out to her.

Taking it, she looked at the earrings on top of the clean dry clothes inside. "You washed them yourself?" she asked, looking up at him.

He rubbed the back of his neck again. "You can tell?"

She bit back another smile. "Thank you."

"I was actually going to come by your hotel tomorrow," he announced.

Her heart skipped a beat. "You were?"

"Yes, to return your things."

"Oh." She looked down at the bag. "Of course. My things."

"And to tell you that I was wrong," he said.

She looked up again. "You were? About what?"

"I don't *not* want to be your friend," he said. "Ever since I dropped you off yesterday, I've been regretting the way I acted and I'm sorry. I want you in my life."

"I want you in my life too," she said, and he smiled, but she forced a frown. "But I can't be your friend."

His smile faded. "You can't?"

Unable to hide her smile any longer, she placed the bag and her purse on the floor next to the couch, raised her left hand, wiggled her ring finger in front of him, and smiled. "Well, not *just* your friend."

He gaped at her. "Did you…?"

She nodded. "It dropped like a stone."

Grinning, he took a step toward her, but she stepped back. He took another step, and she stepped back again.

"You can't kiss me," she said.

"Why not?"

"Because you've already done that." She took another few steps back.

"So have *you*," he said.

"Yes, but I'm changing the rules."

He sighed. "Then will *you* please kiss *me*?"

She shook her head. "No."

"You drive me crazy." He smiled.

She smiled. "You drive me crazy too."

His smile touched his eyes. "You're different," he said.

"Good different?"

"Yes."

She took a small step toward him.

"I think you're ready to hear it now," he said.

"You're finally going to tell me what I said at La Fosse?"

"Yes."

She took another small step toward him.

"We were sitting at the bar," he said, "and you'd just told me about your divorce and how your friend was practically forcing you to get rid of your wedding ring by giving you this trip."

"I said that?"

"Yes."

She took another small step forward.

"Then you told me how alone you felt. It didn't seem like you were in the least bit excited about being in Paris. You said that you had planned to see everything the tourist websites had suggested, in the five days you were here, and *that* would keep you busy so you wouldn't have to think about being alone in a place you didn't know." He tucked the hair in behind his ear. "So I asked you why you would come to Paris if you didn't really want to. You said that your friend had been telling you for months that you didn't know who you were, and that you needed to find yourself. And then you said—"

"I just wanted to see if maybe I was in Paris," she said.

"Yes."

She took another small step forward.

"You remember?"

"Some. I also now remember that *you* then said that—"

"I'll help look for you."

She smiled.

"Does this mean you've found her? The *you*, you were looking for?" he asked as he glanced over her transformation, stopping on her ringless left hand.

"I think so."

He looked into her eyes again and grinned. "It's going to be fun getting to know her."

"For you and me both," she said, also grinning.

"Yes."

Taking another step, she stopped about three feet away from him. She felt a cool breeze against her skin and she glanced at the open balcony-door, only then realizing that it had started to rain again. She looked up at him. "If I kiss you now, can I stay?"

He smiled. "Yes."

She took the last step, leaving only a few inches open between their bodies. Reaching up, she brushed her index finger over his lips, and he breathed in and closed his eyes. She smiled and pushed her fingers through his hair, stood up on the balls of her feet, leaned in, closed her eyes, and softly pressed her lips to his.

Breathing in his sandalwood scent, she slowly parted her lips, and he touched the small of her back while matching the unhurried movement of her mouth.

She trembled and pulled back. Opening her eyes, she

looked into his and then lowered her heels to the floor. Taking his hand, she smiled at him, and then led him toward the steps.

Opening the door, she stopped for a moment and glanced back at him before letting go of his hand and stepping into the bedroom.

She stopped at the foot of the bed, but didn't turn around. Not even when she felt his fingers graze her left shoulder and she trembled again. She didn't turn around when she felt his breath on the back of her neck just before his lips brushed the skin behind her left ear. But she breathed in deeply when she felt him run his fingers over her collarbone and up the back of her neck. When warmth spread through her limbs, she turned around, meeting his eyes.

He took her hand and then leaned down, brushing his lips over hers.

Every inch of her body tingled and she sighed. Pushing her fingers through his hair, she gripped the back of his neck, pulled him toward her, parted her lips, and deepened the kiss.

Kristal looked up at Tyce, who laid on his side with his elbow propped up on the mattress, grinning as he stared at her.

It was still raining, and she couldn't remember ever feeling so relaxed. "What?" she asked softly, not able to hide her smile.

"I could write an entire song about just your eyes," he said. "Pools of silver with a shimmer of blue."

Her cheeks heated.

"And another about this part here." He ran his fingers over the indentation between her collarbones. "And this part." He grazed the skin on her chest where the black sheet covered her naked breasts. "And this," he said, running his fingers over the sheet and down her side to her waist. Moving his fingers over her hip, she breathed in deeply when he touched her thigh where the sheet ended.

Pulling the sheet down, she stopped his hand. "You have a lot of songs to write," she said and pulled his hand up, looking at his palm. "You better rest your hand then." She traced the thin lines with her index finger.

He breathed in deeply and then slowly exhaled. "Now, how are you able to do that by just touching my hand?" he asked and grinned.

She smiled, pulled his hand down to her face and softly kissed his palm.

He frowned. "What happened?" Gripping her right hand, he turned it over and looked at the bandage on her wrist.

"Oh, right," she said. "I forgot about that. I got a tattoo."

"You did?" He looked surprised. "Can I see it?"

She gently pulled the bandage back, revealing an eight-point star with three daisies, positioned in the shape of an upward triangle, in the middle.

"Do you like it?" she asked.

He grinned. "I do, but what do you think your dad's going to say?"

She frowned. "What?"

"Well, you told me that he's pretty conservative."

She gaped at him. "When did I tell you about my dad?"

"At La Foss," he said. "You told me about your dad, your mom, and your grumpy grandfather." He smiled. "I think you said that he would have a stroke if he heard you speaking English. Apparently, he's not a fan of the British."

"Don't worry, I didn't inherit his prejudice." She grinned and brushed a strand of hair out of his face.

He sighed. "But I think I'd like your grandmother best, she sounds like Mrs. Claus by the way you described her."

"She *is* amazing," Kristal said. "But since you know so much about me, tell me something about you."

"Like what?"

"Anything."

He frowned. "There's not really much to tell."

"Oh, I doubt that Mr. I-received-a-highly-acclaimed-humanitarian-award-from-the-city-of-London."

She could've sworn she saw him blush before he answered, "Wow, that's a lengthy title. How do you know about that?"

She grinned. "I Googled you."

"You Googled me?"

"Is that weird?"

"A little, but I'm flattered."

"So, what did you win the award for?"

"Just a music program I started for kids in London." Brushing his fingers over her cheek, he leaned down and kissed her.

When he pulled back a few seconds later, she frowned. "You don't like talking about yourself, do you?"

He smiled. "You never told me what the fifth thing on your list is."

She grinned. "I'm not sure you're ready to hear it."

"Let me guess," he said. "It's '*fall for a handsome musician*'?"

"No, but I'm definitely adding that to the list."

He leaned down and kissed her shoulder. "Tell me," he mumbled while gently moving his lips over her skin to her neck.

Breathing in deeply, she placed her hands on his bare chest and pushed him back. "I can't talk while you're doing that."

"Sorry," he said and rolled over onto his back, placing his hands behind his head.

She turned onto her side, pushed herself higher up on the mattress, and looked down at him. "It's '*Make passionate love to a Parisian*'."

He arched his eyebrows. "So that's why you came over?" He forced a frown, pretending to look angry, "To use me for sex?"

Grinning, she moved her fingers over his chest and

down his right side. "As far as I know, you're from London," she said, tracing the black lines of his tribal tattoo.

He stopped her hand when she grazed the skin near his bellybutton. "As far as *you* know."

She frowned. "What do you mean?"

"I was born in Paris."

She gaped at him. "Are you serious?"

He smiled. "Yes, my family only moved to London when I was six." He placed his hands on her hips, rolled her over, and pushed her into the mattress. "However, I think if you look closely at your list, it says, '*Make passionate love to a Parisian, twice*'."

She giggled. "I'm sure it does."

He lowered his head, stopping his lips an inch from hers, staring into her eyes. Her smile faded when she felt his hand gripping the top of the sheet, slowly pulling it down. His fingers grazed the skin between her breasts and down her stomach to her bellybutton. Her breathing became shallow and her heart started beating faster and faster the farther he pulled the sheet down. She closed her eyes and felt his breath on her lips. Moaning briefly, she arched her back, and then pushed her lips against his. He leaned into her, exploring her mouth with urgency.

Sixteen

"Are you hungry?" Tyce asked, standing against the black-marble kitchen cabinet in a pair of blue boxer shorts, waiting for the coffee to brew.

"Just the coffee would be great, thanks," she said, her legs dangling off the barstool as she leaned her elbows on the counter, watching him. She was only wearing her panties and his yellow t-shirt, with his scent still lingering in the material.

Soft light streamed in through the windows, enveloping the living room. It had stopped raining but it was overcast outside, and she loved that.

Pouring the coffee, Tyce picked up the two cups and walked over to the counter, handing her one.

"Thank you," she said and carefully took a sip of the black coffee.

He pulled one of the other stools closer, sat down opposite her and took a sip from his cup.

"So tell me more about your music program," she asked.

He placed his cup on the counter, cupping it in his hands. "Well, the main aim is to get kids off the streets.

We give out a few scholarships each year. I have people who run it for me but I like getting involved as much as possible. I really enjoy working with the kids when I'm not with the band."

"Children do tend to creep into your heart when you're not looking, don't they?"

"Do you enjoy teaching…what's your language called again?"

She grinned. "Afrikaans."

He repeated the word, and she snickered at his pronunciation.

"Don't make fun of me," he said.

"I'm sorry, but you can't tell me that you don't think my French is funny."

He smiled and reached his arm across the counter, taking her hand.

A shiver ran up her arm when he stroked the wrist of her left hand, and she cleared her throat. "Yes, I enjoy teaching," she said and took another sip of her coffee. "But I'm not sure if I want to teach Afrikaans in Jacobsdal for the rest of my life. I feel like there's something else out there for me. I feel like I have some options now."

"Speaking of options…"

She frowned when he looked serious all of a sudden.

"Do you *have* to leave tomorrow?" he asked.

Her stomach turned. She had forgotten that she was booked on the early morning flight, Paris to London, London to Johannesburg, and Johannesburg to Bloemfontein. "I do," she almost whispered as a lump stuck in her throat.

He looked disappointed. "Can't you move your flight and stay a few more days?"

"I can't," she said, hating the words. "School starts again next Monday but the teachers have to be back on Thursday for prep work."

He looked down at her hand and stroked the tips of her fingers. "So, what are we going to do about this?"

She never thought beyond the point of just being with him, and she only now realized that it might have to end soon. His life was in London and hers was…

For a second the words *'with him'* popped into her head, but she knew they were wrong. She wasn't going to base her happiness on a man again.

She sighed and took another sip of her coffee, glancing at the tattoo on her wrist as she placed the cup down. No, she didn't need him to be happy, she was Kristal; strong, independent, spontaneous, Kristal. She did not *need* him. Then a smile formed on her lips. But she *wanted* him. She squeezed his hand. "Come with me."

He looked at her. "What?"

"Come with me to South Africa."

He frowned. "Are you sure?"

"Not at all, but I *am* sure that I want to get to know you better."

He grinned. "I was just thinking the same thing."

She grinned. "You were?"

"I was. My original plan was to go back to London

on Friday, but I can shuffle some things around." He stood up and walked around the counter, stopping next to her. "We can worry about figuring out the rest later," he said. "I just want to be with you for as long as possible."

"I was hoping you'd say that."

Leaning down, he placed his hands around her hips and lifted her off the chair and onto the counter. Her knees pressed against his stomach and she leaned forward, pushing the hair out of his face.

Lowering his hands, he trailed his fingers over the skin on the outsides of her legs and then gripped her knees.

She grinned, pushed her fingers through his hair and cupped the back of his neck.

At the exact moment that he pushed her legs apart, she pulled him toward her and forcefully pressed her lips against his, parted his lips with her tongue, and leaned into him.

A few seconds later, he tightly gripped her hips, lifted her off the counter, and the moment her feet touched the floor, he swung her around and pushed her against the wall.

His kisses became urgent as he took hold of her arms below her elbows and pushed them up over her head. Her heart raced when he pulled his lips from hers, and she breathed in deeply when he lowered his head and kissed her neck.

Pushing her wrists together, he used his one hand to

pin her hands to the wall above her head, and then lowered his other hand, pushing it in underneath her shirt, grazing his fingers around her bellybutton.

She moaned when he ran his fingers over the skin just above the elastic band of her panties. And when he pulled his head back, she smiled for a second, and then pushed her lips against his again.

"Do you think she's sleeping?" Tyce asked softly as he stood in the doorway of Kristal's hotel room.

She glanced back at the dark room with the drawn curtains, and then placed her purse and the bag with her clothes on the floor. She was wearing her black jeans and blue camisole again, and the clothes she had worn the day before was bundled in the bag. Tyce had lent her the same leather jacket she'd worn when he'd dropped her off at her hotel the last time.

"What time is it?" she asked.

Tyce pulled his cell phone from his jeans' pocket and pressed the button. "Half past four in the PM."

Kristal pulled the black sleeve of Tyce's leather jacket up to her elbow, reached around the corner and pushed the light switch.

"Happy belated birthday!" Zenelda yelled when the lights came on, and Kristal jumped.

Colorful helium balloons filled the entire room, and a large cake stood on the desk next to a bottle of champagne and three flute glasses.

"What did you do?" Kristal asked, gaping at Zenelda.

"I felt bad that I didn't get you anything for your birthday."

She hurried over to where Zenelda stood by the small couch, dressed in blue jeans and a dark blue t-shirt with the words '*When Life Gives You Lemons – Rock On!*' printed in white on the front. Throwing her arms around her, Kristal squeezed as tightly as she could. "You've already given me enough for a lifetime," she said and pulled back. "But I would love to have that necklace back."

Zenelda smiled and pulled the necklace with the sapphire pendant from her jeans' pocket. "I was hoping you'd say that."

Turning around, Zenelda fastened the chain around Kristal's neck.

"Thank you," Kristal said and saw Tyce awkwardly lingering by the door. She walked over to him and took his hand. "Come in."

"No, wait." He rubbed the back of his neck. "I'm sorry that I missed your birthday yesterday," he said and squeezed her hand. "But look in the jacket pocket."

She frowned, reached into the pocket and pulled out a small white box. "When did you get me a present?" She gaped at him.

"Saturday," he said. "I was waiting for midnight to give it to you. But then, well, you know."

She looked at the box and then smiled up at him. Taking hold of his t-shirt, she pulled him down to her,

"Thank you," she said and kissed him.

Zenelda cleared her throat. "Are you going to open it or what?"

Pulling back, Kristal glanced at Zenelda, who was lighting the candles on the cake. She lifted the lid of the box and stared at the white face of the analog wristwatch with the black numbers and the white rubber strap.

"This one's waterproof," Tyce said.

Looking up at him again, she smiled. "For the next time we take a dip in a fountain?"

"Sure." He returned her smile, and then leaned down and kissed her.

Zenelda cleared her throat again, louder this time. "If you two are done making out, come blow out these candles before they melt the cake."

Tyce helped Kristal to fasten the watch around her left wrist, and then he kissed her again briefly before Kristal pulled him over to where Zenelda stood, waiting by the desk.

"Here, you open this," Zenelda said and handed Tyce the bottle of Champaign.

Tyce smiled. "Besides throwing a surprise party, what have you been up to, Zenelda?"

"Didn't you hear, apparently its Zee now," she said and glanced at Kristal.

He frowned. "Okay. So, what did I miss?"

Zenelda grinned and squeezed Kristal's hand. "Maybe one or two things."

Kristal smiled and squeezed back.

"Make a wish," Zenelda said.

"There's really nothing else I could want," Kristal said and counted all thirty candles on the cake before closing her eyes. "But I do wish that I could've completed my list," she said, and when she heard the cork pop, her eyes flew open, and she leaned down, blowing out all the flames in one breath.

"Happy birthday!" Zenelda yelled again and hugged her tightly.

Tyce filled the flute glasses and handed Zenelda one. He handed Kristal the other one, holding onto it for a moment as he leaned down, and kissed her again. When he pulled back, he whispered, "Happy birthday."

Kristal smiled and clinked her glass against theirs.

Zenelda gulped down her drink and looked at Kristal with a mischievous grin on her face. "So, which tasks on the list haven't you completed yet?"

Feeling her cheeks heat up, she glanced at Tyce for a second, and then cleared her throat before looking at Zenelda again. "Getting a mime to speak."

Zenelda grinned. "That's the only one?"

"Yes."

"When did you sing in front of more than fifty people?" Tyce asked.

"It's a long story," Kristal said.

Zenelda smiled. "She performed with Marshall Lovette at the concert last night."

"What?" Tyce gaped at her.

Kristal grinned. "Okay, maybe it's not *that* long."

She took his hand. "I'll tell you about it tomorrow. It's going to be a long flight."

Zenelda's smile faded. "What?"

Kristal turned to her. "*We're* flying to South Africa tomorrow morning."

Zenelda's jaw dropped. "We are? Boom!"

"No, I meant…" Kristal looked at the excitement in Zenelda's eyes. "Aw hell, yes *we* are." She turned to Tyce, who grinned at her.

He raised his glass. "To Jacobsdal."

Zenelda raised her glass. "To all three of us in Jacobsdal."

Kristal smiled. "May the heavens help Jacobsdal."

Both Zenelda and Tyce had insisted that they upgrade her ticket to business class, and as they sat down in the large comfortable seats, Kristal glanced back through the open blue curtains, separating them from coach, and saw the large bald man squeeze into his seat in the second row. She waved at him, but he merely frowned and then leaned back in his seat, closing his eyes.

"You're not going to believe this," Tyce said when she turned back and saw him looking at his phone. "That video of you, singing with Marshall Lovette, has gone viral."

"You Googled me?"

"You Googled me first," he corrected as he pushed his fingers through hers, leaned over, and kissed her.

She breathed in deeply when he ended the kiss, and then she saw Zenelda grinning at her.

"I still can't believe what you did last night," Zenelda said.

"I know," Tyce agreed and looked at Zenelda. "She's really something else, isn't she?"

"Not even I would've thought of doing *that*," Zenelda said, looking impressed.

Kristal tried to hold back a grin, but she couldn't. "Hey, I got that mime to speak, didn't I?"

"You're still surprising me," Zenelda said.

Opening her purse, Kristal pulled out a small folded piece of paper, "Well, let me surprise you one more time," she said and leaned over, handing it to Zenelda.

"What's this?" she asked.

Kristal smiled. "Five things you have to do while you're in Jacobsdal."

1. *Eat biltong*
2. *Learn to ride a bicycle*
3. *Skinny-dip in the Riet River.*
4. *Host a braai.*
5. *Sokkie with a Boer (in front of at least 50 people).*

The End

About the Author

Lize Jacobs was born and raised in Pretoria, South Africa, where she still resides. Although this is her first publication, she has been writing since she could remember, not knowing that being a writer was who she truly was.

She has worked in the video industry for many years; Producing, Directing, Filming, Editing, and Scriptwriting. But her love for film has allowed her to Produce, Direct and Write several acclaimed short films over the years.

Privileged enough to have been able to travel overseas, to places like Alaska, Mexico, Tuscany, Munich, Paris and several African Countries, she has discovered a love for other cultures and the stories hidden in foreign locations.

She is passionate about the diversity and influence of dialogue and celebrates the art of story-telling across all genres.

Her aim is to keep publishing and write film scripts, telling stories which can linger in a person's soul for a little while, hopefully bringing some joy.

www.lizejacobs.com

@lizejacobsbooks

www.facebook.com/lizejacobsbooks